cat's meow

* A Novel *

melissa de la cruz

ILLUSTRATED BY
kim demarco

SCRIBNER PAPERBACK FICTION
Published by Simon & Schuster
NEW YORK LONDON TORONTO SYDNEY SINGAPORE

SCRIBNER PAPERBACK FICTION
Simon & Schuster, Inc.
Rockefeller Center
1230 Avenue of the Americas
New York, NY 10020

SCRIBNER PAPERBACK FICTION and design are trademarks of
Macmillan Library Reference USA, Inc., used under license by
Simon & Schuster, the publisher of this work.

For information regarding special discounts for bulk purchases, please
contact Simon & Schuster Special Sales at 1-800-456-6798 or
business@simonandschuster.com

Designed by Colin Joh
Set in Goudy Old Style

Manufactured in the United States of America

5 7 9 10 8 6 4

Library of Congress Cataloging-in-Publication Data
De la Cruz, Melissa, 1971–
Cat's meow : a novel / Melissa de la Cruz ; illustrated by Kim DeMarco.
p. cm.
1. Young women—Fiction. 2. New York (N.Y.)—Fiction.
3. Fashion—Fiction. I. Title.

PS3604.E43 C38 2001
813'.6—dc21   2001020467

ISBN 0-7432-0504-9

For Mike Johnston

acknowledgments

This book would not be possible without the following people: my wise and patient editor, Doris Cooper; my fabulous co-conspirator, Kim DeMarco; my tireless agent, Stacey Glick at Jane Dystel; the indomitable Hint party patrol: Lee Carter, Horacio Silva, and Ben Widdicombe.

I would also like to thank Airié Dekidjiev, Jessica Jones, Todd Oldham, Tim Blanks, Tom Dolby, Simon Doonan, Michael Musto, John Strausbaugh, Andrey Slivka, Geoff Kloske, Kathleen Cowan, Liza Sciambra, Amy Larocca, Jennie Kim, Mindy Schultz, Caroline Suh, Ellen Morrissey, Thad Sheely, Gabriel Sandoval, Ruth Basloe, Alicia Carmona, Peter Edmonston, Andy Goffe, Gabriel de Guzman, Tristan Ashby, and Tyler Rollins for their friendship and enthusiasm.

Last, I extend heartfelt thanks to my family: Bert and Ching de la Cruz, Francis de la Cruz, and Steve and Christina Green, whose love and support have been invaluable.

You're a slave to fashion and your life is full of passion . . .
But you keep asking the question
One you're not supposed to mention
When will I, will I be famous?
>   —Bros, "When Will I Be Famous?"

I've learned a tremendous amount from maids in my life.
>   —Diana Vreeland, *DV*

contents

12 *CONTENTS*

PART THREE: KINGDOM COME

EPILOGUE: THE AFTER-PARTY

avant le déluge

1. *introducing the quixotic cat*

My name is Cat McAllister. Tonight I will celebrate my twenty-fifth birthday for the fourth time. Things I like: birthdays. Things I don't like: liars.

I'm the kind of girl who laughs loudly, smokes incessantly, and appears to be hell-bent on destroying herself, but *stylishly*. Really, I should have tragically overdosed by now. Or else succumbed to some harrowing disease brought on by vodka tonics and Tic Tacs. So the least I can do is *refuse* to age gracefully—to defy it every step of the way, just like Melanie Griffith.

I used to be famous—well, maybe famous is too strong a word. I began my career as the smiling baby on the side of the Pampers box, an auspicious beginning considering Jodie Foster started out as a bare-bottomed Coppertone kid. But unlike Jodie, whose preeminence in Hollywood began through roles in movies like *Taxi Driver*, *Freaky Friday*, and *Stealing Home* (a rare stumble), and who ultimately garnered double-fisted Academy Awards, I auditioned for the role of Gertie in *E.T.* but ended up the poor man's Punky Brewster. My specialty was variations on orphan roles: on *Miami Vice* I played a spunky street urchin, on *Growing Pains* the Seavers' stray before Leonardo diCaprio usurped my role with that bowl haircut and dimple of his, and on *Webster,* where I became lifelong friends with Emmanuel Lewis. The apex of my career came when I starred in my very own network vehicle. I played the precocious adolescent adopted by Pat Morita and Dyan Cannon, but our little "dramedy" failed after one season. Apparently the world wasn't ready for *Party of One.*

As a teenager, I was set to reign as the Gisele of the day—the ruling model of Paris, London, and Milan—but instead I became an Asahi beer calendar girl in Tokyo. In fact, I'm the sixth Spice. I tripped on my five-inch platforms on the way to the MTV shoot and missed out on the taping of the "Wannabe" video. I'm stuck in that seventh circle of celebrity hell where I'm just recognizable enough that people think they know who I am but on second thought can't place me for the life of them.

Oh, well.

Maybe the reason I turn twenty-five every year is that I feel like I'm in a holding pattern. Because while I've done *almost* everything and been *almost* everywhere and I know *almost* everybody in New York, I'm nowhere on the *New York Observer*'s yearly sociopopularity index. My one consolation is that I own the appropriate wardrobe should Annie Lebowitz ever come calling—a closet full of designer labels, ostrich feathers, fox stoles, tulle underwear, silk kimonos, sequin shifts, and cigarette holders. I even own the pink dress Marilyn Monroe wore in *Gentlemen Prefer Blondes* (Madonna has a *knockoff*).

Things you *won't* find in my closet: shoulder pads, tie-dye, wash-and-wear.

My life just wasn't supposed to be so . . . stagnant. Everyone who's anyone has certainly moved on from the impromptu-striptease-on-the-dance-floor stage—now either glowingly pregnant and happily married while launching their own clothing line or making their directorial debuts at Sundance or overseeing billion-dollar cosmetics companies—the jet set is simply so *talented* now (days of lolling about in chair sedans decidedly over)—but the only thing I seem to have accomplished is the ability to shop while blindfolded. How utterly humiliating to realize that I still haven't made a handsome match while saving the world with a cure for cancer, or at least hosting a benefit for the cause.

It's terribly unfair, because I was *made* for paparazzi stalkers and tabloid headline notoriety. After all, I was born on Park Avenue and baptized just down the street from the holy temple of Bergdorf Goodman. Daddy was an up-by-his-bootstraps kind of guy, a self-made businessman from Queens whose success bought prime beach-front acres in East Hampton. Mummy was a woman of devastating beauty and outlandish charm—she was a flight attendant. They met over first-class cocktails sometime in 1970. Back then Mummy wore a smart little Yves Saint Laurent uniform made of blue polyester with orange trim, but she soon graduated to Saint Laurent couture. Yet for all her efforts to penetrate the Mortimer's–American Ballet Committee–Rockefeller Foundation crowd, Mummy was always too *nouveau* even for the *nouvelle*, who saw her as a vulgar interloper (this was before the eighties, mind). When my father lost a sizable amount of his net worth through a series of bad investments—million-dollar restaurants that never gained more than one star in a *New York Times* review, waterfront property for a baseball stadium that never materialized, a controlling interest in Betamax—she stopped trying to fit into New York society altogether.

I was eight years old when my parents divorced. Daddy found solace in a series of young blondes who didn't seem to mind that he had been downgraded from billionaire to millionaire, while Mummy took up with a succession of men of descending importance in the political and entertainment fields—from Academy Award–winning directors and Republican congressmen to Latin American playboys and Norwegian *parfumiers*. Mummy also retains a marginal hold in the public eye by writing an astrology column for the *National Enquirer*.

*   *   *

I live for velvet ropes and open bars, aviator sunglasses and seaweed scrubs, Hello Kitty lunchboxes, pony-skin handbags, peacock-feathered shoes, and gold-leaf invitations to VIP events. The kind of exclusive fete frequented by glossy-magazine editors, DJs, models, photographers, stylists, kindersocialites, the several pseudo-celebrities "cajoled" into showing up (Gary Coleman, Sylvia Miles, Monica Lewinsky) as well as the legions of assorted fashionable hangers-on—aggressive party crashers who more often than not spend their days manning the M.A.C. counter at Bloomingdale's—star-struck kids with a talent for self-invention who have just arrived in the city from Florence . . . or Fresno.

I'm happy to report I'm booked every night of the week, except on Friday and Saturday nights, of course, when the city is filled with a strange kind of people. Those who hold jobs. Not that my manic partying isn't *work*. That's why weekends are devoted to maintenance and television. It's the only time I can devote myself to *Sabrina the Teenage Witch* and *Popstars*, put on my oxygen mask, and practice my breathing. Sometimes I'll even do all three at once.

So where did I go wrong? In the back of my mind, I always thought that by the time I reached thirty, I'd have *something*: either a rich and successful husband who kept me in couture or else a fabulous and fulfilling job that garnered me the respect and envy of my peers. But instead of ascending up the New York circles via legacy or meritocracy, I spend my days in Madison Avenue dressing rooms and my nights in the unsavory confines of certain nightclub bathrooms. It's all getting to be so predictable and surprisingly tedious, and loneliness, as Bryan Ferry croons, is a crowded room.

Perhaps I should mention that my erstwhile fiancé, Brockton Moorehouse Winthrop the Third, or "Brick" for short—recently broke off our on-again-off-again engagement. He dumped me for a Victoria's Secret supermodel. One Pasha Grigulgluck—otherwise known in the press as the "Tits from Transylvania." Pasha was a high school dropout and runaway from the national figure-skating team. Two months and two silicone injections later, "nineteen"-

year-old Pasha was pouting down from a billboard on Times Square and had my ex-boyfriend wrapped around her little finger.

Brick is a polo-playing venture capitalist, an extremely busy and successful man. We dated on and off for years. Oh sure, we rarely *saw* each other—he was always racing his hot-air balloon somewhere over Uzbekistan while I was shopping on Carnaby Street, but that was the point. We kept in touch via speakerphone—Brick would dial me from his Gulfstream V, so his voice always sounded vaguely far off, as if he were some kind of god. But I don't really miss Brick as much as I miss the *idea* of him.

India says I'm being silly, because how can I be lonely when I have her in my life? India Morgan Beresford-Givens is New York's reigning postoperative transsexual. In other words, a drag queen who's *gone the distance.* She's also my best friend in the whole world. India swears she's descended from the Astors, as well as being a bastard cousin to the British royal family. Her life has been one of scandal, intrigue, painful hormone treatments, and invitation-only Chanel sample sales. I've known India forever. We've gone from New Wave groupies with asymmetrical haircuts and Duran Duran fixations, to clown-suit-wearing club kids in ski masks, to Gucci-clad fashionistas tripping over nail-heel stilettos. India doesn't understand loneliness, mostly because she never sleeps alone. I, on the other hand, can hardly stand the thought of soiling my five-hundred-thread-count Frette.

"Cat, is something wrong?" India asked, horrified. "You've hardly touched your vodka tonic." We were having our usual late-afternoon liquid lunch at Fred's, the restaurant in the basement of Barneys.

"I know," I mourned. "What's wrong with me? I detest angst. I've *done* angst. I've been to college."

"What you need," India chided, "is a new man. Look at me, I feel fabulous. Invigorated." India had a new man every other week. "You've got to stop whining about Brick and the supermodel. You need something new—more specifically, you need *someone* new."

"But who?" I asked, hiding behind oversize sunglasses that used to belong to Jackie Onassis. India knew as well as I did that I was hopeless when it came to men. My relationship with Brick lasted for so long because we didn't have real conversations. Brick was the King of the Monologue, and expected the Nancy Reagan treatment at all times. I highly suspected I didn't really want a man—not for all the typical reasons, anyway. I wanted a "handbag"—something that would look nice on my arm. Sometimes I wished I could just skip the whole relationship thing and proceed straight to the alimony checks. So much easier that way.

"Well, obviously, it's got to be someone worthy. You can't just end up with some regular Joe Schmoe off the street," India said.

"Obviously," I agreed, rolling my eyes at the very thought.

"What about a de Rothschild? A Whitney? A Vanderbilt? A Whitney-Vanderbilt? A Rockefeller?" India threw out last names like clothing labels—which wasn't too far off, when you thought about it. A Louis Vuitton lifestyle funded by a princely American fortune—isn't that what a modern Manhattan marriage was all about? Except all the new billionaires were over in Silicon Valley, and God knows I would never move there. I mean, where would I have my hair done?

"Darling, doesn't your mother know anybody nice?"

I gave India a look.

"Oh, that's right, dear. I keep forgetting."

My mother flitted about so much, exchanging men like foreign currency, that the only way to keep track of her movements was by consulting an international collection of dubious celebrity magazines. "There was a small mention in *Paris Match* about some sort of birthday party for her pet poodle last week," I said. Sometimes I did receive the occasional cablegram inquiring about my health. Mummy on e-mail? She didn't even know how to dial long distance!

But it was useless to complain, as Mummy did what she could. For my fifth birthday, she threw an authentic barnyard bash—at the Waldorf-Astoria, just like Elsa Maxwell—complete with real animals—cows, pigs, goats, and chickens. "But, madam, we cannot have livestock in the ballroom!" the scandalized concierge had protested. But they did, by custom-making felt slippers for the animals' hooves. The hit of the party was Elsie the cow, who milked champagne and vodka from her udders.

"I've got it!" I said, quaffing my cocktail in a gulp, finally understanding what it was I really wanted in a man. "*Von und su!*"

"The right possessive pronouns," India agreed, impressed.

"A little *Thurn und Thaxis.*"

"*De* or *du.*"

"Or better yet—an 'of Something'! Not even a last name—just a country!" I was *inspired.*

"With an HRH in front."

"Hmmm . . ."

"Hmmm . . ."

"But what about—egads, HRH Princess Marie-Chantal of Greece?" I asked.

"Err—it does give one pause." India nodded.

"But I suppose I could live with it," I decided. "I've got it! Stephan of Westonia," I said, remembering a recent conversation with social gadabout Cece Phipps-Langley.

"The Royal Prince of Westonia?" India asked, cocking an eyebrow. "Hmm . . . could be a good prospect. And not bad-looking either, even with the eye patch."

"Oh, it's all about the eye patch," I said. "By the way, where is Westonia exactly?"

"Somewhere in the Baltic, I think, near the Balkans. Or is it Bavaria?" India mused.

"Cece said he keeps homes in Buenos Aires, Baden-Baden, and Beverly Hills . . . and that brokers are taking him to look at penthouses on Fifth Avenue and beachfront cottages in Sag Harbor," I said. Cece never gossiped about anyone who wasn't important. "Apparently his title dates back to the Holy Roman Empire and he can trace his ancestry to all the royal houses in Europe, the imper-

ial court of Russia, as well as Oliver Cromwell, Napoleon, Franklin
Roosevelt, and, um, Serge Gainsbourg."

"So what does he do now?"

"Mmm . . . I don't know for sure. Some sort of financial thing
with a Wall Street bank, I'm sure. Don't they all? Supposedly he has
gazillions. Not one of those all-castle-no-cash kind of things. He's
only thirty-five and—get this—unmarried," I said in a breathless
rush.

"And he's not gay?" India asked keenly.

"No, I don't think so. Cece said he just came out of a secret relationship with Princess Caroline."

"Of Monaco?" India asked, impressed.

I nodded eagerly.

"Well, then, how . . . serendipitous indeed." We silently contem-
plated this minor miracle. Rich. Titled. Single. Straight. *Parfait!*

"And you know what they say. A good man possessing a great
fortune should soon be parted from it through marriage," I said to
India. "Or something like that."

Was it Socrates who said an unexamined life is not worth living?
Possibly. But as the advent of a twenty-four-hour Reality Channel
(which broadcasts the minutiae of ordinary people transplanted
into extraordinary circumstances, the reward of surviving their
ordeal a seat on David Letterman's couch) has proved, it's an
undocumented life that's not worth living. If one's every move isn't
gossip-column fodder or fan-website worthy, does one even matter
in the grand scheme of things? And darlings, I wanted to matter. I
wanted to matter very, very desperately. Therefore: Stephan of
Westonia. My ticket out of B-list obscurity. Understand, it's not
that I really wanted to be married. Prenuptial agreements and
clothing allowances just weren't my style. Look at what four mar-
riages did to Patricia Duff. OK. Bad example. But you know what I
mean. If I were somehow able to position myself as Stephan's bride,
I would ratchet up the ranks faster than you could say Gwyneth
Paltrow.

"What do you think?"

"You know what I've always thought," India replied. "You'd be perfect for Bill Gates, if only he were divorced, or JFK Junior, if only he were still alive, or Rupert Everett, if only he weren't gay. But since there's no other option, I approve."

"But how do I meet him?" I asked. It's not like I bumped into exiled royals at Barneys all the time.

"What about a party? Isn't it your birthday soon?" India asked. "I do enjoy celebrating your twenty-fifth every year."

Oh, of course, of course. What better way to attract New York's most dashing bachelor than at a dazzling birthday party feted by a chorus of celebrities? I was getting thrills up and down my back just thinking of it. It was going to happen. Even if I had to bankrupt my trust fund to pay for it. I'd just explain to my accountant that it was an investment in my future.

I would send my mother an invitation to my birthday party, but knowing her, she won't be able to make it and would merely send along a nice card and a check for $20 for "a glass of bubbly."

Who I am: Cat McAllister. One of *People*'s fifty most beautiful people (1982).

What I do: live in the *moment*.

What this book is about: me, silly!

2. plus one

There must have been a time, long ago in Manhattan, when birthday parties were something of a private affair—maybe a corner table at Elaine's with one's family, and if well-wishers like Barbara Walters and Liz Smith *happened* to stop by, it was only because they were dining there that night. That's not the case anymore. Everyone from Kate Moss to Jennifer Lopez to the Olsen twins has the kind of birthday party that merits national media coverage and the usual trappings of a colossal social undertaking: clipboard-wielding attack girls, VIP rooms, even corporate sponsors.

Thanks to Heidi Gluckman, the one-woman publicity genius who made dining in supertrendy restaurants serving bad food and outrageous attitude a full-contact sport in Manhattan, I was going to host the Mercedes-Benz Cat McAllister Fourth Annual Twenty-Fifth. Heidi had all the qualifications of her profession: she was blond, incomprehensibly accented, and had all the city's top gossip columnists on her "secret" payroll.

Pay Heidi enough money and you, too, could be a star. On a dare, she once transformed a common shop girl into one of the city's most visible socialites. It got to the point where the shop girl began to believe in her own tear sheets—so much so that she actually stole a bona fide socialite's husband. So if Heidi could turn a hayseed into Holly Golightly, why not a pseudocelebrity into the real thing? This was going to be my comeback of sorts—the coronation of a new Manhattan diva!

It's terribly important to leverage successfully an appreciation of one's "brand" in society. As I explained to Heidi, I wanted to position myself as the "people's socialite." Less tragic than Jackie Onassis, more accessible than Babe Paley, more substantial than Carolyn Roehm—able to leap large puddles in a single stiletto bound! After all, the media loved extravagance—who could forget Malcolm Forbes's million-dollar birthday party on a private island, complete with calvary charge? Or Saul Steinberg's, in Quogue, which included tableaux vivants of his favorite Flemish paintings? If Heidi succeeded—and she would—my birthday party would bring immortality—or at the very least a mention in the party pages of *Vanity Fair*—hmmm . . . maybe Mummy would even see it.

Heidi's plan for my fantabulous fete required a crew of several hundred cater-waiters, a reception tent, and the services of a top society florist whose showroom spent several weeks crafting American Beauty roses out of delicate silk ribbon. The party would be the perfect setting for an introduction to the mysterious, handsome, eye-patch-wearing exiled European prince.

The guest list was limited to five hundred of my closest friends. The party was to be held at the hottest club of the moment. The hottest club of the moment is understood to be a club that hasn't even opened yet—to the public, at least. It's gotten so bad that Keith McNally's latest venture, which opened when Madonna was still in her Indian charka phase, still has an unlisted reservation number today. I briefly considered a place that was so new it was still a sweatshop! "Garmentos will love it!" the club's publicity director promised. "Set up the bar next to the sewing machines—so Kathie Lee ironic! And don't worry about the Chinese women—they'll be gone by ten P.M."

Tempting, but I decided to pass. I thought it best to head for less edgy pastures. In the end, I decided on a fail-safe option, a club owned by a consortium that included the New Jersey Mafia, a Colombian drug lord, and a former celebrity money manager.

But first: an outfit. The right dress is integral to any event—it sets the tone, it makes a statement—but what statement did I want to make? A demure Giorgio Armani beaded evening gown? Or a thigh-high dress with matching panties from Donatella Versace? Perhaps I could cajole my personal shopper at Gucci to send me *the* plunging-neckline silk jersey dress that everyone would be wearing *next* year. Or perhaps I could wear a little something from Alexander McQueen, it was sure to be insane. Choices, choices! Finally, I settled on an outfit that was flattering as well as politically loaded—a mini-chador, the latest rage from European runways. Plus it was just the thing to wear with Catherine Deneuve's djellabah.

My standard hours-long preparation involved a meditation tape, a disco nap, and practicing bons mots with my personality coach. When I was finally perfumed, moisturized, sanitized, and depressurized, I slipped into my couture chador. It was difficult to see out of the thing—much less use a cell phone. But as Debbie Harry says, true beauty involves suffering. On my way out, I called India from the car.

"Are you just about ready? We're here in front of your building. Do you need me to come up?" I asked. India lived two blocks down from me, but we never walked to each other's apartment. That's what Lincoln town cars are for! (*Stretch* is *très* gauche!)

"Oh, do come up, darling," she replied. "I'm just about done."

When her maid let me into her apartment, I was shocked. India was still in her bathrobe, her wig in electric curlers—an affectation she picked up from Andy Warhol, who used to get haircuts for that white mop of his.

"Darling!" I squealed, agonized. "You lied! You're not ready at all!" I started to panic. Very soon, I was expected to blow out some candles in front of a rather large and varied crowd of New York's most unforgiving social butterflies, at a party that was sure to launch me out of *TV Guide*'s "Where Are They Now?" shadows and into the **bold-font** universe. After all, I'd paid Heidi dearly to secure Dominick Dunne. Since mine still wasn't a name people recognized, Heidi had to wrangle in celebrities the old-fashioned way.

She lied to them.

She told the Miller sisters the Lauder sisters had already RSVP'd, told the Boardmans the Ronsons were definitely going to be there, and once the word got out that both Aerin and Samantha were definites, everyone else fell in line: the de Kwiatkowskis, the Hiltons, Marina Rust, Ahn Duong, Brooke de Ocampo, Eliza Reed, etc., etc., etc. She told *Vogue* that *Harper's Bazaar* was going to be there, told *Harper's Bazaar* that *Vogue* was sending three of their editors. She told 'N Sync *Cosmo Girl* was sponsoring the party, told *Cosmo Girl* that 'N Sync would throw a free concert, and now the band was scheduled to serenade me at midnight! Heidi's staff even dropped hints that Madonna was my new best friend. Thanks to her masterful machinations, the prince's arrival was all but a lock.

"Oh, calm down," India soothed. "It won't be a party without you. Really, don't be ridiculous. We've got a lot of time. Now let me look at you," she commanded.

I twirled around in my gorgeous robes, gauging her reaction by peeking out of the eye slit.

"Gorge!" she enthused.

"Reverse chic!" I pronounced.

"Fashion oppression."

"So low it's high."

"So bad it's good."

"So clean it's . . . dirty!"

"As Andy Warhol would say—Wow."

"You think?" I preened.

"Simply *beyond*," India declared.

"Genius!" I agreed, pulling a Diana Vreeland. Things we like:

DV, Diana Vreeland's autobiography, Liza Minnelli in *Cabaret*, irrelevant references to historical fashion icons. Things we don't like: *Prozac Nation*, cowboy boots, plus-size models.

"Now, darling," she commanded. "I've got a bottle of gin on my dresser. Why don't you be a sweetie and make us drinks?"

I checked my watch. Hmmm. We did have some time. And I did want a drink to calm down. My stomach was aflutter at the prospect of talking to Puff Daddy. I never had anything to say to him, and "Who's suing you now?" seemed terribly rude. A few preparatory cocktails were certainly in order.

"First, help me out of this thing. It's rather stuffy in here. I don't know how those models manage it," I said, taking off my hood.

India and I first met in Tokyo. I left Hollywood at thirteen when my sitcom was canceled, and by default—since Daddy didn't seem to mind and Mummy was off in Monte Carlo for the season—I declared myself an Emancipated Minor just like Drew Barrymore and left for Japan to make my fortune. But I didn't go to record bubble-gum teen pop, like Jennifer Love Hewitt. I went to model.

Back then, India was still allowed in the men's room (and certainly nothing stops her today). Tokyo was a relatively minor market for models in the early eighties. It was where they sent you if you weren't tall enough to work in New York or Paris, but were pretty enough to convince the Japanese to buy car wax and Asahi beer. I lived in the Shinjuku section with several other girls in a "model apartment," bunking with a fifteen-year-old redhead from Puerto Rico and a seventeen-year-old corn-fed blonde from Iowa. Deanna rolled her r's and could drink anyone under the table. Staci was a Miss Iowa State Fair and determined to become a spokesmodel. By the time I arrived the two of them already had their share of *yakuza* boyfriends and brushes with horny French photographers. I lost my virginity during my first photo shoot, with a nineteen-year-old from Grenoble. Jean-Luc had dark hair and a way with a camera. He retouched the photos of me to make it look as if I were wearing no underwear, then sold them to a skin mag. Welcome to Tokyo.

I spent most of my time shopping and hanging out with touring American rock bands. I'd throw druggy, five-day parties, rent motor scooters, and spend my weekends smoking pot in Bali. With Daddy's monthly allowance checks, I was able to float this lifestyle for several years since I made almost no money from modeling for magazines like Portuguese *Vogue* and North Korean *Cosmopolitan*.

India lived next door to us. A narrow youth of nineteen, back then she looked not unlike a Japanese animé character, with a platinum pixie haircut, bad skin, yellow teeth, and an oversize floppy head supported by a scrawny little body. I would have *killed* for her waistline. She professed to have only her education to thank for her androgynous appearance. India was the product of a British public school, an institution firmly entrenched in nineteenth-century ideals. Gruel, corporal punishment, and substandard heating were *de rigueur*, resulting in a student body of underfed, malnourished, and anorexic boys. Who needs Leptin? Just send the obese over to jolly old England! After flunking her O levels, she hightailed it to Japan, where she auditioned to become the frontman for a Japanese New Wave tribute band called Barbarella Ballet. They played Depeche Mode covers and Yaz synth-pop. The Japanese kids in her band were beside themselves. Who needed Haircut 100 or Kajagoogoo when you had India in blue eye shadow and a ruffled poet's shirt? She was hired immediately.

India saved my life in Tokyo. It turned out my roommates were routinely signing checks on my already overdrawn account, leaving me with an eviction notice and foreclosed on the motor scooters. I was too embarrassed to ask Daddy for help, although I did try to contact Mummy, but she was living in Iran with the Shah at the time and had her own problems. India was the one who saw me through it all—lending me enough money to buy an airline ticket back to New York and hiding me in her apartment before the Japanese police could find me and throw me into their . . . educational system. I was having warm, nostalgic thoughts about that time when India broke my reverie.

"So have you thought of what you're going to say to Stephan?" India asked as I pulled the stays of her corset tighter. Urrrgh. Scarlett O'Hara and Mr. Pearl could boast eighteen-inch waists but India surely did not.

"What about 'hello'?" I asked. How hard could it be? Bat eyelashes. Drop handkerchief. Find oneself at Harry Winston.

"Darling, you're going to have to do better than that. You know, Cat, the art of small talk is sorely underrated," she chided.

"It is?" I panicked. This whole seduce-and-destroy theory was getting too complicated for my liking. With Brick I hadn't needed to do any of that. When we met I was eighteen, winsome, and his girlfriend's best friend—a true turn-on for the ages.

"What does he like? What turns him on? What doesn't?" India mused. "You're going to have to play geisha a little bit. Remember to laugh at all his jokes and to have subjects of conversation that are light, topical, and will hold his interest," she said, sounding like a headmistress at finishing school.

Oh, dear. I was never good at playing the enraptured coquette and as far as I was concerned, geishas belonged in Japan. Shopping was so much more gratifying than sex, anyway. I mean, don't get me wrong, I *like* sex. I just can't abide *mess*. With Brick, I scheduled our intimate moments in between a strict regimen of enemas and meditation. Romance was an icky-smelling Ralph Lauren perfume, and I always had more fun in a Manolo Blahnik boutique than the boudoir, anyway.

"Now, what do we know about Westonia?" India lectured.

"Um, nothing?" I ventured.

"Right," India agreed. "Boot up the computer, darling. You can find everything on the Web these days."

Keeping my fear of carpal tunnel syndrome at bay, I logged onto India's iMac and surfed for any information regarding the kingdom of Westonia. "There's nothing," I griped after several failed attempts. "And we're getting late for the party.

"Oh, wait, here's something. It's his personal home page!" I said, excited. Stephan-of-Westonia.com included hyperlinks to illustrated maps of the country, which looked like it was located somewhere in the Austro-Hungarian hinterlands near Greece, Turkey, Bosnia . . . and Moldavia? The map was awful fuzzy and hard to read.

"Darling, do you think he might be related to Catherine Oxenberg?" I mused. "Isn't she some sort of Eastern European princess?"

India shrugged.

I continued to click on the links. "Here's something about his family." There was a very small picture of grim-looking people wearing tiaras. "Apparently they were thrown out of the country in the revolution of 1918. The royal family was shepherded into some farmhouse and massacred. Only a son survived—Wilhelm the Second. And like a lot of deposed royals, he relocated to Argentina. Stephan is his great-grandson and the heir to the throne. Except there isn't a throne anymore. There's a military junta. Oh, this is all so fascinating."

"Anything else?" India asked.

"No." I checked again. Apart from the map of Eastern Europe and the small picture of the doomed royal family there was nothing.

I checked the time again. Oh, no! We were late! I put on my chador and hustled India out of the apartment. As a last-minute confirmation, I rang Heidi just to make sure everything was under way for my grand entrance.

"Is everyone accounted for?" I demanded. "Richard Johnson? Rush and Molloy? Aileen Mehle?"

"*Oui,*" Heidi said crisply.

"Aerin Lauder? Li'l Kim? David Blaine?"

"*Ja.*"

"Stella McCartney? Plum Sykes? George Wayne?"

"*Sí.*"

"And what about," I asked breathlessly, "Stephan?"

"Mmmm . . ."

"Excuse me, I didn't quite hear you, Heidi."

"Ah . . ."

"Stephan?"

"Ahhh . . . haf bad noose, Caf," Heidi groaned. "Stephan ees coming. *Mais, ploos on!*"

Stephan of Westonia PLUS ONE. A date! The Westonian prince had RSVP'd for my party with a date! A guest! A plus one! It was bad news indeed. It seemed the most eligible bachelor in New York was not so eligible after all.

"Plus one!" I moaned.

"A mere technicality," India tut-tutted. "This is Manhattan, my dear. Every woman worth her Vuitton waiting list has her heart set on that man. The debutantes are sharpening their manicures as we speak. Surely you didn't think this would be easy, did you?"

"You're right; of course you're right."

I was about to follow her out, but passed a hallway mirror on the way. Aiiieeeeee!!! Who *was* that black shroud? Momentary panic as realization dawned, then turned into a paralyzing flash of fashion self-consciousness! Le shroud *c'est moi!* I mean, I've always dressed outrageously. When John Galliano ushered in "homeless chic" for Christian Dior I was all for it—donning a tattered newspaper dress and stringing it with empty Coke bottles. I've had to enter door-ways sideways because of my addiction to Philip Treacy's monu-mental hats. But perhaps Muslim chic was not the smartest choice for the evening? Could it be possible that instead of looking like a fantastic, gorgeous, right-off-the-runway fashion phantasm, I looked like nothing more than a Bedouin goat farmer? Eeeek. This would not do at all!

"I'm going back home to change," I told India. "You go on ahead."

3. good help

I went home to ransack my closet—there had to be something other than layers of black silk to wear to The Most Important Night of My Life! I put on Greta Garbo's fur coat, Sammy Davis Jr.'s tuxedo, even Marlene Dietrich's fishnet stockings—but everything was too fussy, or not festive enough, or else had belonged to a dead celebrity with horrible body odor. In desperation I called for Bannerjee. Bannerjee Bunsdaraat is a twenty-one-year-old Sri Lankan medical student and my gal Friday. Tonto to my "Sloane" Ranger. Alfred to my Bruce Wayne. She's my au pair.

Which means that she keeps meticulous track of all my clothing purchases, arranges my vast collection of haute couture pieces, as well as oversees the RSVP process chez McAllister. The secret of professional partygoers is a handy little mimeographed book called the Fashion Calendar. Published every two weeks, it lists every affair *de la mode*—from the complete roster of fashion shows and after-parties to splashy magazine launches to mundane trade fairs. Party whores like myself, who don't necessarily work in but,—ahem—*appreciate* fashion are made to justify our presence by harassing beleaguered PR agents. But persistence pays off—with my status as a former child "star" I can usually scam invitations for up to five parties every evening. Of course, this means that sometimes India and I find ourselves at some loony private corporate shindig for the "new panty line" (the Warnaco party) or else an awards dinner celebrating the "I Am Beautiful Awards" with Marlo Thomas. Note this is a real event.

Bannerjee's task is to fax an infinite amount of invitation requests to event organizers and then sort the invitations that arrive afterward. Banny knows to discard the ones unimaginatively scheduled on a weekend night, and RSVP's a yes for everything else. She also coordinates appointments with my manicurist, pedicurist, facialist, herbalist, and nutritionist so they don't arrive all at the same time and confuse me. Otherwise I'd have my face waxed and my toes exfoliated. As a special treat, Banny also makes sure there's fresh air in my water wings for my daily bath.

Oooh. Where is she? Usually at this hour Banny is steam-cleaning my cashmere sweaters or else in the kitchen, highlighting *People*. If they gave out Ph.D.'s for celebrity trivia, Bannerjee would chair the department. She knowingly refers to one of Cher's ex-boyfriends as Rob "Bagel Boy" Camiletti. When John-John was killed, Bannerjee fasted for a month and left copious amounts of flowers, poetry, and a beloved teddy bear at the vestibule of his apartment. She's since transferred her affections to Prince William, whom she likes to call "Wills." Unfortunately, not only does "Wills" live in England, he's bound by law to marry a virgin, preferably of the same race and class. But like I said, Bannerjee is nothing if not persistent.

She told me how she ended up in New York as an au pair. During her last year of medical school in Sri Lanka, a benevolent and wise old aunt who worked as a housekeeper on the Upper East Side told her she could make more money taking care of children in the United States than she would ever do so as a doctor in her tiny little island village. "You go to America," her auntie Punjabi had suggested. "You be au pair. You have fun. You go to parties. Meet American boys. No worry about baby. Put in front of TV. It's what

Amerrrycans do ennyway." It was just as her aunt had predicted. And since I didn't have any children, her job was even easier than most au pairs'. Bannerjee keeps me company on shopping trips. This leaves her more than enough time to participate in multiple orgy sessions with Swedish busboys from downtown nightclubs or whatever else au pairs do in the city on their nights off. Which reminds me. Lately I've been getting calls confirming RSVPs for my "long-lost Sri Lankan cousin." Apparently this person is named Bannerjee also. *Quelle* coincidence!

I'm so proud of Bannerjee. She so quickly acclimated to the stringent requirements of living in New York. She orders my cigarettes from the corner deli, is well versed on taxicab culture, and has mastered the art of impeccable dressing.

I was beginning to get very annoyed, as I couldn't remember if I had given her the night off. I didn't think so. Oh, dear. I hoped she hadn't been kidnapped or anything. I shuddered. When I was younger my greatest paranoia was that I'd have my ear cut off and mailed to my father. At college, it was of being abducted by the Symbionese Liberation Army and brainwashed into wearing full-body jumpsuits and a beret. Not that I had anything to fear now that I was practically bankrupt. Sigh. There was no sight of her. And unfortunately so much of my clothing demanded an extra hand—I certainly didn't know how to artfully arrange a scarf on my chest all by myself. I was a total klutz when it came to nipple tape!

The chador would just have to do. Besides, I remembered that I had eschewed my daily salon blow-out because of the head covering. There was no choice but to soldier on. Bedouin goat farmer or not.

I wondered if India had noticed my prolonged absence when I realized my cell phone was vibrating. So that's what I'd been feeling for the past half-hour. I thought maybe I'd suddenly developed Parkinson's. *Très* relief! I flipped it open underneath my hood.

"Darling, where are you?" India cried. "Everyone is waiting!"

It was India. I was loved! I was missed! My heart felt full even if my hair felt sweaty.

"Sweetie!" I gulped for air. "I couldn't find a thing to wear and Bannerjee's missing!"

"Oh, for godssakes, it's your party. Hurry up or you'll miss the laser-light show. I'll send Heidi to the door to make sure you get inside."

By the time I arrived it was after midnight, and a crowd of fabulous nobodies had already converged at the nightclub doors. Heidi had envisioned a two-tiered event: champagne dinner for an elite group (Tina Brown, James Brown, Foxy Brown) and a raunchy after-party for the rest of the free-drink faithful (lifestyle reporters, soap-opera actresses, one-hit wonders).

I walked confidently to the glossy gatekeeper. "Cath Marlister," I said.

"Who?" She gave me a skeptical look.

"Thuthus mff parffy. Mmm Cath Marlister."

She flipped through her clipboard. "I'm sorry, Cath Marlister is not on the list. Is there another name you could be under?" she asked, faux-helpfully. What was going on? Why couldn't they recognize me?

"Mfff Heidi around?"

"I can radio Heidi," the doorbitch finally agreed, and pretended to speak into her headset. After a minute, she said, "Heidi says you are entitled to paparazzi clearance. You're right here." She motioned to the roped-off police-barricaded section *outside* the club where photographers were stationed. Prime real estate for taking pictures of incoming celebrities, but several hundred feet away from the VIP lounge and a three-tiered birthday cake.

I started babbling desperately, and a man who was leaving the club with a woman who was giggling loudly stopped on his way out to see what was the matter. "Are you all right . . . miss?" he asked doubtfully. I couldn't see him very clearly as tears were welling up in my eyes, but he seemed tall—and he smelled great.

"Hey, now, what's going on here?" he asked as I made mewling sounds underneath my chador.

"Oh, nothing, everything is fine . . . she's not on the list," the Clipboard Nazi answered airily. "Party crasher, probably," she said *sotto voce*. "Anyhoo, thanks so much for coming! Don't forget your goodie bag!" she trilled, handing him a brightly colored paper bag decorated with origami cats, which contained several travel-size "sponsor gifts" that Heidi was able to corral: a CD from an unknown band that shared a manager with 'N Sync, sample-size bottles of body lotions, an assortment of hair gel and mini-lipsticks, all products represented by her PR firm.

"Let the poor thing in," he said in an accent I couldn't quite place. "There's no harm."

"Sir, please be reasonable. She only has paparazzi clearance" was the nasty reply.

"Getttfff MmmHeidi . . ." I gurgled.

"Heidi? You need to see Heidi?" he asked.

I nodded eagerly.

The woman by his side tugged on his arm. "Let's go, darling . . . c'mon, we'll be late for the next party," she complained. Her voice sounded familiar, but I couldn't hear very well underneath my chador.

Just then I spotted Heidi at the door, frantically searching the crowd for any sign of me. I waved. "Heidifff MmHeidiff!" Finally it dawned on me: the chador! Not only was it muffling my voice, it was keeping me from being recognized at my own party by the very people I had employed to keep out the riffraff!

"Caf?" Heidi asked doubtfully, looking in my direction and peering into my dark veil. "Vhat on earrt?"

"Muslim chic," I explained.

Heidi nodded. She herself was wearing a dress with an immense Gucci ruffle that threatened to decapitate her. We exchanged careful air kisses and she instantly whipped open the velvet rope. I turned around to thank the nice man who had tried to argue my admittance, but he was gone. Mmmm . . . pity. Wonder if he was cute? Heidi quickly ushered me inside, stopping for a moment to lecture her employee. "Zees is Caf McAllithair! Caf, I am so, so sorry," Heidi said, apologizing profusely. The woman groveled as I walked past her, whining, "But Miss Gluckman, she said she was Cath Marlister and her name wasn't on the list! Miss McAllister, I'm so sorry. Can I get you anything? Your hood? A cocktail?"

Once inside, I was shocked to find the nightclub strangely empty. Oh, sure, the usual cadre of junior editors, A&R music reps, photographer's assistants, and hairstylists were networking madly, hammering back flutes of champagne, but I spied no one of note. No one **boldface** worthy. Something was *horribly* wrong.

"Is Puffy still here? Has Madonna left? What about Li'l Kim? And Aerin Lauder Zinterhofer?" I asked desperately. "The cake— the candles—the 'N Sync serenade? You didn't blow out the candles yet, did you?"

Heidi looked contrite. "Ah, so sorry, Caf, vous wair trop laite, zee crowd vus gaiting ressless. Peeple started leeeffing, so vee had to go ahead und celaibrate vour virthday viffout vous."

"Excuse me?" Unless I was wrong, Heidi was trying to tell me they had gone ahead and celebrated my birthday without me. It just didn't seem possible!

"Don't vorry. Eet vus svectaculair."

"But how?"

"Vail, ziss voman zay, zhe und Stephan cunnot vait anymoore. Zow, zhe blue candles. Vantastic. Lazur-layt zhow. Kek. 'N Sync seroonade."

"Where is she?" I agonized.

"VIP lounge." It was the only thing Heidi pronounced correctly.

On my way upstairs to confront the person who had benefited from all my birthday planning and to give her a piece of my mind— unless, of course, it was someone *important* like Chloe Sevigny; then I'd just laugh it off and we would become girlfriends. Wheee. But now what was this? As I arrived inside the darkened confines of the VIP room—a cramped roped-off area in the back—and my eyes wandered around the assembled Arab potentates, twenty-two-year-old dot-com CEOs, NBA athletes, voluptuous R&B songbirds, and several princes of extinct foreign states (but no Stephan in the bunch), who did I bump into but my missing-in-action au pair, Fedora-wearing gossip columnist to her right, cigar-chomping investment tycoon to her left!

"Bannerjee!" I shrieked.

"Miss Cat!" she gasped. "It's terrible, Miss Cat!"

Terrible didn't *begin* to describe it. Bannerjee was wearing the Helmut Lang parachute-silk pantsuit I'd been made to understand was out of stock at Barneys! And I had *trusted* her with my personal shopper.

It was a particularly painful betrayal.

"I know!" I agreed. "That's just my size and they don't have any more!"

"Pardon, Miss Cat?"

Before I could explain, a piercing wail broke several sound barriers.

"Aiiieeeee! Cat, darling! I tried to stop them!" It was India. She was waving a champagne flute above her forehead and she looked delirious. "They had to arm-wrestle me away!" she declared, hyperventilating. "It was awful! I threatened a *tantrum*—but it was too late!"

So it had really happened—for a minute I had almost convinced myself Heidi was just joking—but, yes, everything had gone off exactly as planned! It had been *svectaculair*—just as Heidi had promised! But I didn't want to believe it—didn't want to face the awful truth—that I'd actually *missed* the best party of the season— *mine!*

"So who blew out the candles? And where's Stephan?" I demanded.

"He's gone." India sighed. "He left."

"But with who—where?"

"Oh, sweetie," India said, embracing me in her large, muscular arms. "You really don't want to know."

It was just too much. I fell to the floor, slipping through my friend's grasp and hitting my head on a gilt-edged table, knocking cocktails onto a gaggle of assistant stylists fighting over the last of the hors d'oeuvres. And then—nothing. I felt wind rushing toward me. Was I flying? Was this what death felt like? Should I go toward the light?

Later I found it was only Bannerjee fanning me with part of my djellabah.

4. bankruptcy, barneys, and public humiliation?

The phone woke me just as my head hit the pillow the next morning. I had yet to recover from the evening's exploits, which included a raucous impromptu birthday celebration at La Goulue. After picking me up from the floor, India and Bannerjee took me to my usual banquette, where we whooped it up with Ivana Trump and Count Roffredo Gaetani, who were under the mistaken impression that India was Jocelyn Wildenstein.

I reluctantly answered the phone, if only to stop it from ringing.

"Miss McAllister?"

"Yefff?"

"This is Miss Walters from Citibank. Miss McAllister, I'm calling regarding a problem with your account?"

Shit! Shit! Shit! I'd taken to se-habla-españoling when creditors called, or else advising them gravely that "Miss McAllister" was out of town, out of the country, or even dead. But this early-morning phone call had caught me off-guard. Why, oh, why, hadn't I checked the Caller ID?

"Uh-huh?"

"Yes, well, according to our records, your accounts are severely overdrawn. Will you be able to make a deposit this week? Otherwise, we're going to have to charge off your accounts, and I don't think you want that on your credit record."

"Uh—OK. I'll call my accountant. Did you say *all* my accounts are overdrawn? Can't you take money from my savings or CD or IRA accounts to cover it?"

"We did that last month, Miss McAllister. You've cashed in your IRA, and your savings and CD accounts are down to zero. Meanwhile, your checking account is in negative figures, and your credit account is over the limit."

Beep!

Beep!

"Oh, I'm sorry. Can you hold?"

"N—"

Click.

"Hola? Como esta? No habla inglés," I said in a desperate attempt at an authentic Spanish accent.

"Cat! Cat! It's me, darling! Why are you speaking Spanish? Don't you know Ricky Martin is over?" It was India. Why was she calling me so early? India was rarely conscious before happy hour.

"No—it's not. I'm just—it's—well—what do you want?" I asked irritably. I was never in a good mood when I was awakened with bad news about my financial situation—which lately was every day.

"Darling, have you seen the papers?"

"No." I checked at the foot of the bed for the stack of newspapers Bannerjee collected for me every morning. Strangely enough, they were not in their usual place. "Banny!" I called. "Could you bring me today's papers, please, sweetie?"

"Oh, no. Tell her not to. Perhaps you shouldn't," India said worriedly.

"Why not? Oooh . . ." I said excitedly, a sudden thought forming. "Is it all over town that I missed my own birthday party? *Please* tell me no . . ."

"No."

"No?" Huh! Must check with Heidi if she alerted the usual press syndicates. I harbored the smallest hope that at least the party would be mentioned, even if I wasn't there to enjoy it. Then, suddenly, it all came back to me: my arrival post-candle-blowout-and-pyrotechnic display. And most important, I had missed the *raison d'être* for the *cause célèbre*—the all-important introduction to the prince!

Bannerjee entered carrying the *Post*, the *Daily News*, and the *Times*. She had a troubled look on her face, and tiptoed out the door after depositing them on my bed.

"So why did you call, then?" I asked India.

"Oh, nothing, darling. Nothing at all, don't worry about anything . . ."

"But I am worried!" I wailed. "I've got terrible news!"

There was an immediate, shocked silence. Then: "Oh. My. Lord. Tom Ford is dead!"

"No, no, no. Nothing like that."

"Oh, thank God." India breathed a loud sigh of relief.

"It's terrible, just terrible!" I cried, agonized. "I've got Citibank on the other line—my accounts are overdrawn!"

"Oh, that again?" India asked in a been-there, bankrupted-that voice.

"No, this time it's different."

"How?"

"You know how much that party cost me! And I haven't received a check from my trust in several weeks," I whispered desperately.

"Why don't you just call your accountant and ask for your check?"

"I'm scared to," I whimpered. "What if—what if—there isn't any more?"

"Any more what?"

"Money."

"Oh, darling, don't be silly. There's always more money. Probably just a blip in the system. Maybe it's a latent Y2K bug. Nothing to worry about, I'm sure everything will work itself out. You're not broke. How can you be broke? Rich people never go broke. Look at Michael Milken."

"What about you, darling, you're broke?" I said thoughtfully.

"I am a scion of a crumbling British estate. We've been broke since the fourteenth century. By now, it's tradition," she said. India paid for her lifestyle by doing freelance styling gigs for artsy fashion magazines around town, and the rare cocktail lounge act, singing those good old New Wave tunes, and to my understanding she was also not adverse to accepting large amounts of money from a certain generous patron who preferred his ladies to be of the transsexual variety. "But you Americans are never really bankrupt—you're just experiencing negative cash flow," she said.

"Are you sure?" I asked.

"Positive," India soothed.

"Anyway, I suppose I could call my mother if worse comes to worst," I said lightly.

"Oh, of course. Where is she again?"

"Well, there was a picture of her at the Save Venice ball," I said. "But then I think I read in *Manhattan File* that she was off to the Bahamas. I suppose I could always leave her a message in Palm Beach, she's sure to end up there . . ."

"In September . . ." India said doubtfully.

"Three months from now . . ." I finished. It was useless. By that time, I could be living out of a box! This was just like my first year in boarding school, when I was the only child who arrived sans underwear and a toothbrush because Mummy had forgotten to pack them.

Yawwwn. "So what are we doing tonight?" I asked, changing the subject. I didn't like to think of myself as neglected so much as indulgently brought up with minimal parental supervision. I shuffled the papers idly, flipping through the New York *Post*—thousands murdered in the Bronx, political campaigns-ho-hum—ah, here it was. Page Six.

"AAAACCCKKK!"

I dropped the phone in horror, then examined the rest of the papers hurriedly. But it was all the same!

Bannerjee entered the room at the sound of my voice. "Miss Cat!" she said fearfully.

"Cat, what's wrong? Cat, are you still there?" India called from the receiver.

I ignored both of them. It appeared Heidi had done her job after all. There it was—*my party*—the lead item above the Sean Delonas cartoon! The club was described as "exhibiting a post-apocalyptic grandeur not seen since Club USA opened in Times Square," and the list of boldface names ran the gamut from Justine Bateman to Dweezil Zappa. Strangely, there was no mention of Aerin Lauder, Li'l Kim, or Stella McCartney—how could these intrepid reporters have missed them? Still, it was everything I'd dreamed about—except for one key detail. Precious column inches were devoted to describing the actions of one Teeny Wong Finklestein Van der Hominie! "Hello to the New Downtown Diva" read the headline. "Intended for a birthday celebrant who never showed up, the brazen but lovable fashionista-socialite Teeny Wong Finklestein Van der Hominie ended hours of waiting by taking it upon herself to daintily blow out the candles on a frosted pink birthday cake. 'Well—I *am* good at blowing,' she giggled as an SRO crowd impatiently waited for the laser light show to begin."

It got worse—accompanying the text was a picture of Teeny arriving at the party on the arm of Stephan of Westonia. She had been his plus one! Needless to say, that was as close as I came to getting any press for my birthday. Was this public humiliation? Gross public indifference was more like it. Even Liz Smith, Cindy Adams, and the *Daily News'* Rush and Molloy had run perfunctory mentions about the party, but only because a drunken supermodel had to be carried off the dance floor.

"Cat? Is everything all right?" India asked.

I retrieved the phone from underneath the bed. "Teeny." I cursed. "India—why didn't you tell me?"

*   *   *

As far back as I could remember, Teeny Wong Finklestein Van der Hominie had lurked behind each one of my monumental failures. Teeny stalked the runways of Paris while I made do with car commercials in Japan. Teeny won an Emmy for her portrayal of *The Girl Who Spelled Freedom* while I starred in failed sitcoms. Teeny, whose visage was the face of mannequins in the Costume Institute, Marianne of France, and the Trinidad and Tobago ha'penny! Teeny, who had introduced my ex-boyfriend Brick to the Victoria's Secret supermodel. If I hadn't been on Xanax I'd have felt practically murderous.

Teeny was a social climber of the worst kind—a successful one. She didn't have friends—she had sponsors, sycophants, and handlers. We met in junior high, in between my Hollywood coming-of-age and the subsequent modeling stint in Japan. Teeny was loud, exuberant, ambitious, and cheated at Monopoly. In Beverly Hills she was best friends with Monica Lewinsky *and* Tori Spelling. Teeny played both ends of the popularity game. She adored me so much that she consistently updated her own wardrobe according to my purchases. Every birthday and Christmas, Teeny would wait until I sent over the requisite Lucien Pellat-Finet sweater or token from Fred Segal, only to reciprocate with a gift that matched, to the last dollar amount, the exact cost of my gift to her. Teeny boasted an infinite knowledge of discounts and sample sales, and once when I placed an Impostors ring in a Bulgari box, Teeny responded with an ABS dress with a Versace label.

Much worse, Teeny was insufferably vain and even more insufferably gorgeous. Married at nineteen to a dentist from Scarsdale, she divorced him at twenty-one and moved back to New York with a hefty alimony. For years, she was just another divorcee partial to bluebloods with blue-chip stocks, but that ended when she married a ballet dancer who was also the heir to a mammoth Austrian fortune. There were rumors that the union was less than . . . how should I put this? Consummated. But no doubt Teeny would land on her feet in the arms of another, richer man. She was that breed of female more commonly known as a "guy's girl," in that every man who had ever met her was immediately charmed into thinking she was the sweetest, most innocent, involuntarily-but-devastatingly-sexy woman who wouldn't wish ill on a fly. Her male defenders numbered *Manhattan File*'s Hot 100 Bachelors list. But girls knew better. Teeny would steal your husband in your borrowed dress. Just ask several well-married debs who have lost managing-director-husbands to this upstart.

What was hardest to swallow was that Teeny was also prosperous in her own right. Unlike other Park Avenue heiresses who let their fortunes slip through their fingers . . . *ahem* . . . Teeny, a born-again Christian, parlayed her Machiavellian skills and generous inheritance into a flourishing line of moderately priced polyester imitations of the latest designer fashions. Her Tart Tarteen label continually sold out in malls across the country, and was patronized by a gamut of young Hollywood starlets, including the entire roster of the WB network. I absolutely abhorred Teeny.

But the thing is, I just wasn't built for confrontation. It made me queasy and off balance. Hair-pulling-knock-'em-down-all-out tussles were for tough chicks who wore pancake makeup and Revlon lipstick. On the other hand, I felt weak in the knees when my slashed-elbow Helmut Lang sweaters pilled. I was the type of person who was unfamiliar with complaint departments. I never sent back food in restaurants, no matter how badly overcooked was a plate of "raw" tuna. I preferred that things not be "uncomfortable."

I mean, sure, I harbored fantasies of ripping Teeny's spine out of her ass and of sticking my fingers through her eyeballs, but this was real life, not claymation. If I really wanted to hurt Teeny, I'd have to switch her black market Phen-Fen capsules to fat pills. Then I could let it slip to certain gossip columnists that Teeny had a history of sexually transmitted diseases. But the absolute worst thing I could do to a girl like Teeny was to make her poor. Unfortunately, there wasn't much I could do about Generation Y's buying power, or teenagers' predilection for ersatz couture.

Teeny was the kind of girl who was always in the spotlight—and she had stolen my moment away from me.

This would not do. This would not do at all. I felt dizzy and weak—overwhelmed by the magnitude of my failure and missed opportunity.

"India—meet me at Barneys, fourth floor, now," I said in a strangled voice.

"Right."

I set down the phone. "Banny—send for the car."

Before I left, the phone rang but this time I let the machine answer it. "Miss McAllister, this is Ms. Walters from Citibank. Please call me back to arrange payment on your overdrawn accounts."

Overdrawn schmoverdrawn. This was an emergency! Citibank be damned. I still had my *Amex* card.

5. charity begins at home: the china syndrome

Darling, I do think I feel right as rain," I said to India as we perused the minimal racks, pulling out crinkled Issey Miyake shirts and bulky Dries Van Noten sweaters. "It's amazing how . . . medicinal this all is. I've almost forgotten about that hideous party."

"Mmmmm," India agreed. "Thank God for unlimited credit limits."

Party poopers like Overspenders Anonymous will tell you that shopping is a disease. An addiction—something that leads to an overstuffed closet full of collapsed clothes racks and, say, fifty plastic storage bins full of Fendi bags. By my last count I owned 350 pants in the same color (black) and a collection of seventy-five white T-shirts—clothes that I *can't even wear* because the last time I tried to pull out a pair of pants the rack *fell on me*. So of course they're right—it *is* a compulsion—otherwise, where would be the *fun*, I ask you—but I never really regarded it as a *problem*. Problems are things like the Middle East and starving children in China. Shopping is merely a sport.

Barneys is the shopping decathlon. It takes energy, concentration, and an honest perception of what your body can handle. The weak-willed and the self-delusional need *not* apply. Now, I asked India, as I walked out of the dressing room to stand in front of the three-way mirror, what is your honest, honest opinion of my butt in these Alexander McQueen bumsters?

"An excellent choice," a low voice drawled.

I turned around and almost bounced out of my bumsters. India was nowhere to be found—probably lost in the black hole that was the Manolo Blahnik boutique—and instead standing in front of me was the exiled prince, His Royal Highness, Stephan of Westonia himself! He was indeed nice-looking, especially with the eye patch. Tall, with somewhat craggy features but a handsome solidity. Broad shouldered. And wearing the most heavenly narrow-cut wool suit with a beautiful spread collar. Mmmm . . . and he smelled delicious, even familiar.

"You're going to want to wear them this way," he said, coming up behind me and putting his hands squarely on my hips and tugging down at the waistline. "There, that's better," he said, stepping aside.

"You think?" I asked coyly, pursing my lips and examining my reflection in the mirror.

"Definitely." He nodded, appraising me from head to toe, his gaze finally settling upon the litter of chic black shopping bags piled at my feet.

"Do you always come up to strange women at Barneys?" I asked flirtatiously.

"Oh, I'm sorry, if you'd like I can—"

"Darling, I'm just joking. I'm Cat McAllister, I don't think we've been properly introduced," I said, offering my hand.

"I'm—"

"Oh, I know who you are," I said airily. "I mean—you're

Stephan, aren't you? You were at my birthday party the other night."

"Uhmm . . ." He looked flustered, and peered from side to side worriedly, as if on the lookout for a hidden photographer.

"Oh, don't worry," I assured him. "It's Barneys. They don't let paparazzi in."

He smiled. "Indeed, they don't. I'm sorry, what party was that again?"

"It doesn't matter." I shrugged, thinking he probably went to five parties a night. "It's just not every day a girl turns twenty-five for the fourth time," I said coyly.

He laughed. "I'm sure I would remember that. Wait a minute . . ." His brow furrowed. "By any chance, were you wearing a chador that evening?"

"Me? A chador? Nooo! Of course not. Fashion oppression is so . . . last week," I declared as I bumped into a store mannequin wearing the exact replica of my birthday party outfit: veil, hood, and all. Even the matching tie-cord sandals.

"I see." He nodded enigmatically. Mmmm. He did smell nice— and so familiar—*too* familiar . . . It finally dawned on me: he had been the man outside the club who had come to my aid! I swooned, until I remembered how tragic the whole night had been.

"Maybe you'll remember me when we meet at the next party," I said.

His face brightened. "Of course! Monday night!"

"I'll keep an eye out for you," I said gaily, then blushed crimson at the unfortunate pun. Fortunately, he didn't seem to notice.

"Please do."

"What's happening Monday night again?" I asked. "I never remember what's on my calendar."

"The benefit for Chinese orphans? At the Statue of Liberty?"

"Oh, yes, of course," I said, pretending to know all about it. But what I did know was that Chinese baby girls were the latest trendy charity—even more popular than dyslexia or the rain forest. The

newspapers were running daily accounts of Chinese orphans abandoned by the thousands. The babies lollygagged at orphanages for
years, until warmhearted and childless couples from the United
States heard about their plight and came to rescue them. The Chinese Orphan Society of New York was throwing a dinner-dance at
the Statue of Liberty to raise the profile of the cause. Send us your
huddled masses, indeed.

"Those poor things."

"Yes, it just breaks your heart," he agreed.

"Rows and rows of those abandoned Chinese babies. Simply too
triste for words."

He nodded soberly. "A real shame."

"Those sad-eyed tykes. Is there anything we can do?" I asked
him sorrowfully.

"Well . . ."

"I mean, how terribly lonely to grow up in a world without anybody to love you or buy you DKNY Kids clothing!" I agonized.
"Think of it, they're only going to grow up to scrounge around for
food and then get sold into slavery or an arranged marriage. I
mean, you have seen *The Joy Luck Club*?" I demanded.

"Actually—"

"But, anyway—yes, I will be there. Chinese babies. Miss Liberty.
Ahoy!" I cheered. "So . . . Monday night, yes?"

"By all means," he agreed, striding off as my personal shopper
returned with another armful of clothes.

"I think I will take these pants," I said thoughtfully.

"You'll never guess who I bumped into," I told India, whom I found
sitting like an indecisive Cinderella in the shoe department.

"Who?"

"The prince. Stephan," I bubbled.

"*Quel surprise!* Did you speak to him?"

"Speak to him? We had a convo to die for. A meeting of the
minds, darling."

India cocked an eyebrow. "You don't say."

"Oh, he's divine. Even better than the pictures. And that eye patch—it's so rakish, don't you think? Lends him a somewhat dangerous air."

"So what was he doing here?"

"At Barneys? I don't know. Shopping, I suppose.

"But, anyway, darling," I said impatiently. "There's a benefit Monday night for Chinese orphans."

"I know. We respectfully declined, remember?" India chided. "It was twenty thousand dollars a ticket. Good Lord, for that amount of money, you could *buy* yourself an orphan."

"That's it! That's just it! Darling, I'm going to order Chinese," I decided.

"But what about Fred's?" she asked, meaning our usual lunch date.

"No, sweetie. A baby girl. From China."

"What are you talking about?"

"I'm going to adopt a Chinese baby."

"What for?" India asked, aghast.

"Isn't it better to actually show, you know, a personal interest in the cause? He'd be so impressed—it would completely floor him. Besides, everything Eastern is just the thing right now," I told her grandly. "It's spreading faster than the Hong Kong flu."

India shook her head. "Whatever you say." She thought I was joking, of course. But I wasn't. It was time to get serious, and what better way to capture a prince's attention than to make a generous gesture toward his favorite charity? Isn't that what drew Charles to Di? Her love of, um, children?

"Don't you think it's a little . . . well, extreme?" India asked. "Can't you just send a starving child a dollar a day?"

Extreme? Did India remember who she was talking to? After all, I was the woman who, several fashion seasons ago, when prosthe-*chic* had been the height of fashion, had demanded a double amputation just so I could wear Alexander McQueen's latest creation. The British fashion bad boy had outfitted a legless model with knee-length wooden prosthetics in the shape of black boots with intricately carved embroidery. GENIUS! I literally ached for them. Damn legs were simply in the way. So I went to his showroom to be fitted with same. Oh, don't look at me like that. They're doing marvelous things with reattaching limbs nowadays. In France they have just learned how to reattach a man's arm to his body. Thought I'd just keep the legs on ice, like Uncle Walt, then get the reattachment surgery the next season—that was if legs were in style again. I arrived at the showroom, only to be told that it was illegal to amputate someone unless it was a medical necessity. I tried to explain that it was a *fashionable* necessity, and in certain parts of the world—like the one I lived in—it was almost the same thing. So, no—I didn't think adopting a Chinese baby was too extreme, given the circumstances.

"But first things first. About this benefit, how much was a ticket again?" I asked India.

"Twenty thousand dollars."

"Twenty thousand dollars?" I repeated, crestfallen. There was no way I would be able to swing that after today. My eye wandered to the numerous shopping bags.

"Darling—don't!" India cried when she realized what I was about to suggest. "At least spare me the Blahniks!"

I marched India and our shopping bags up to the register. "Sweetie, charity begins at home."

Even if the idea of adoption was an impulsive act—and what rash decision of mine hadn't been?—motherhood was definitely something I'd been mulling over for a while now. I couldn't walk by the second floor of Barneys without cooing over the little booties and baby-size leather jeans in the layette department. India berated me for suffering from a case of urban-accessory envy.

"You only want one because everyone is having theirs," India accused. She was just sore because I made her return a new pair of alligator pumps. "Cindy Crawford. Alexandra von Furstenberg. Madonna. Manhattan is turning into one big nursery. Babies sliding off the catwalk during Fashion Week, being fed lobster sushi at

Nobu, even strapped on the back of hip mama chests at Pucci gallery openings."

"Maybe," I conceded. "But think about it—a little Chinese baby of my very own! For me to love and cuddle and for Bannerjee to feed and burp!" Even if Bannerjee displayed no visible nurturing skills whatsoever, what did it matter? Bannerjee knew nothing 'bout no babies. That's why she was an au pair!

"But, Cat—you're talking about a baby!"

"Of my very own! I mean, it's about time. Don't you think?"

"Is that wise?" India queried. "I mean, a baby is a lot of work, Cat. There's all that spitting up and diapering and then they grow up and stick you in some nursing home. Or worse, eighteen years later you'll find naked pictures of her on your boyfriend's fireplace. Did you ever think of that?"

"Well, no, but I'm sure Bannerjee—"

"Bannerjee is not going to be the mother. You're going to have to take responsibility for this child. And what about your accounts? Can you even afford a child right now?"

"Well, according to yours truly I'm not really broke, anyway," I argued. "Remember? 'Temporary cash flow situation.' 'I'm sure everything will turn out all right.' Besides," I joked, "if I have to go on welfare, I hear they give you more money if you have kids."

Then again, maybe India was right. Perhaps this was a tad premature—but what were my other options? God knows the sight of an epidural needle would send me into shock immediately. And the thought of getting fat! I hadn't been fat since Daddy died. It was a terrible shock, as I'd always thought I'd have more time to get to know my father. A benign if somewhat distant figure of my abbreviated childhood, Daddy was sixty years old when I was born. But he did try—I have extremely fond memories of the time he ordered our chauffeur to teach me how to ride a bike. I inherited everything that was left—the Park Avenue penthouse he'd managed to hang on to, and the East Hampton compound where my grandparents now live, as well as a substantial and, I had believed at the time, unlimited, trust fund. My accountant suggested a plan where he would continue to send me monthly checks from the fund's interest earned, while a broker would be hired to take care of my investments. I agreed to everything without understanding anything.

While I was tempted to sell the penthouse and move downtown to a loft, complete with welding set and Shabby Chic furniture, in the end I decided to stay. Besides, it would have been criminal to leave Mummy's custom-built temperature-controlled closet. Still, it was an awful period. For the first time, I was completely alone. Mummy was in the Caribbean, launching a cruise line. I'd lost touch with the thieving models I knew from Japan. Even India was living in Denmark at the time, reinventing herself. I was a strong candidate for Jerry Springer's fat-people rescue, although I didn't think I exactly qualified for the baby-whale crane. I refused to leave the house in my condition. Ten pounds and a full dress size?

Mummy suggested extreme measures, so I spent six months at an ashram rumored to have been a favorite of the Miller sisters. I did sit-ups and morning jogs and drank protein shakes and kickboxed my way out of obesity. So, no, I didn't think pregnancy would agree with me at all. But this was different. I would be rescuing a little Chinese tot from a life of sure destitution. I mean, they didn't have Helmut Lang in China, did they? I was ripe for motherhood, I could just feel it! Why, the other day I had even stopped to pet a dog, and I'm allergic to animals. This was just what I needed to bring a little meaning to my life. Besides, Stephan looked like the kind of man who would take to the idea of adopting a Chinese orphan—after all, he shopped at Barneys, he would understand. When I got home I called Bannerjee into the room.

"Yes, Miss Cat?" she asked humbly. She was still embarrassed about the Helmut Lang pantsuit incident, and sported a black eye and bruises. Not from me, mind you! She'd hit her head on the sofa when she tripped over the rug going to the bathroom.

"Banny darling, you know how you said you'd do anything for me to stop being mad at you?" I coyly batted my eyelids.

"Yes, Miss Cat. Anything," she intoned breathlessly.

"Well, there is something," I wheedled. "Chinese baby girls, Banny."

"Yes?"

"Well, I want one! Off you go. Go pick me up one."

"Off where, Miss Cat?"

I rolled my eyes. "China, of course! Where else do you find abandoned Chinese babies? They're not giving them away at Pearl River Mart, you know."

"But, Miss Cat—I'm not supposed to leave the country," she protested as I hustled her out the bedroom door. "I don't have a visa."

"Oh, why?"

"I can't leave the United States until I get one. And they don't give out that many—I think the quota has been filled for this year."

"But what does that mean?"

"It means if I leave the country, I might never be able to come back."

"Really . . . how strange. Well, never mind that, I don't have a Visa either. You know how it is," I said, rolling my eyes and mouthing "Maxed over the limit." I strummed my fingers on my vanity table. "Here's my platinum Amex."

Packing Banny off for her great adventure took the rest of the day. After I called the airline and secured her on the next flight to Shanghai, Bannerjee watched helplessly as I threw her sweaters, underwear, jeans, and sneakers into an overnight bag.

"Oh, that reminds me. You know those little pointy hats they wear? Make sure you bring me back one as well. I'm channeling headgear for fall." I zipped up the bag with a flourish. "There you go. Good-bye, Banny darling. Do pick a nice fat one! I'm counting on you!"

After Banny disappeared in a cab, I picked up the phone to dial India. I hoped she wasn't still sore about the reversal of fortune concerning her designer footwear. Luckily, I caught her in an ebullient mood—she had just been with her man of the week, a nineteen-year-old go-go dancer from the Bronx.

"I did it, darling! Banny's off to China as we speak," I announced. I paused for dramatic effect. "You *do* know they're almost out?"

"Of babies?" India asked dubiously.

"No, Visas. But I'm not worried; I gave Bannerjee the Amex. So what do you think? Please tell me you don't think I made a mistake," I begged.

"A little enfant chinois! You know, I suppose it really is quite adorable," India cooed. "Can we take it out and dress it up in those little pajamas?"

"Of course, darling. Why else would I ever get one? I mean, China is just the thing these days. Mu shu pork, chopsticks as hairpins, Jimmy Choo sandals!"

"But don't forget, China also means century eggs, fortune cookies, and Long Duck Dong," India reminded.

"Still, just look at that China Chow."

"China Chow my fucking ass," India exclaimed. "Just because her mother was, like . . . *Chinese.*"

On principle, India and I do not approve of nepotism-acquired fabulosity. We've agreed. One isn't *born* glamorous. One falls assbackward in Gucci stiletto heels to achieve it.

People who are glamorous: Joan Crawford, Jane Fonda, Cher.

People who are decidedly not glamorous: Christina Crawford, Bridget Fonda, Chastity Bono.

"You know, Cat, now that you're going to become a mother, you really are going to have to be more responsible," India chided.

"Oh, of course, of course. Now, did you remember if the party tonight is open bar or not?"

After a night spent in louche dance halls with India and her nineteen-year-old go-go dancer, I had a lovely dream that Stephan and I were walking in Central Park with a little Chinese baby. Just remembering how his one bright green eye twinkled at me made me feel certain I had done the right thing.

6. belle of the ball

The success of a charity ball requires three things: a worthy cause, a celebrity-studded board of directors, and a seating chart that reflects a creative *joie de vivre* as well as an astute knowledge of the guests' complicated public and private lives. For instance, Madonna and Sandra, Kate and Anna, Mercedes and Anne, Carolyn and Marie-Josée, Paul Theroux and V. S. Naipaul, Rosie O'Donnell and Tom Selleck must always be kept at a great distance from each other, albeit at tables of equal importance. I had asked to be seated near Stephan of Westonia, and was therefore distressed when I received the following message on my answering machine:

"Miss McAllister, this is to inform you that you and Miss Beresford-Givens will be seated at Table Z for the Chinese Orphans Benefit Ball."

Table Z? Now, that did not sound right at all. From experience, I knew that if you were seated past table D you were in trouble. I called the committee's public relations firm to inform them that a terrible mistake had been made.

"Hi, this is Cat McAllister, confirming my seating for the Chinese Orphans Benefit Ball?"

"Yes, Miss McAllister. You are at Table Z" was the chirpy reply.

"Table Z?" I asked. "Are you sure? Now, where is that exactly?"

"It's slightly off center."

"How off center?"

"Off-off center . . ."

Only after I dogged her with increasingly specific questions concerning the whereabouts of my table was it finally revealed that India and I had been given seats at a table so far back it was located *behind* the Statue of Liberty. I demanded an immediate explanation.

"Well, you see, you RSVP'd quite late, and we were at capacity. We're sorry, but this is a very small space, and we're already oversubscribed," she said, giving me the rote PR response to any question. If public relations people ran the world, they would duly inform invading space aliens that the planet was "at capacity" and if they had any hopes of securing it, they should have RSVP'd earlier.

"Darling, it's an island!" I protested.

"Yes, but—"

"Never mind. I know, you're at—"

"Capacity," she finished perkily.

Sigh. Some things were just not worth arguing about. Besides, after dinner, I could table-hop as much as I pleased—all the way to Stephan's circle.

The night of the benefit, India and I arrived for the party in coordinating Christian Dior by John Galliano cheongsams. I felt very Sofia Coppola, on the lookout for my own Spike Jonze. The benefit committee had commissioned authentic Chinese junk boats to ferry guests over to Liberty Island. A gauntlet of photographers stood ten deep on either side of the red carpet on the pier. India and I air-kissed a retinue of friends while giving others only a languid "fashion finger"—the common greeting between fashionistas that involves a crooked wave with one's index finger to acknowledge the presence of acquaintances with whom one would rather not be acquainted. Assaulted by paparazzi, Uma and Ethan quickly ducked into an awaiting boat without stopping for a photo op, but others, like visiting British dignitary Posh Spice, were more generous with their time.

India positioned herself next to the most important person on the red carpet, in order to ensure that *her* picture would run in magazines' party pages as well. "Hello, hello, only on this side, please," India ordered, posing with a flourish. "That's India, spelled I-N-D-I-A, Beresford-Givens, B-E-R . . ." India spelled her name twice, checking the reporter's notes when done. Sure enough, three months later, right in the middle of *VF Camera, Vanity Fair's* splashy scrapbook of the rich, famous, and their arm-candy dates at various charity balls, art gallery openings, and glitzy events about town, was the picture of India standing at the pier en route to the Chinese Orphans Ball. Unfortunately, the accompanying text read: "Nan Kempner and friend." *Oh no.* Not *and friend*! India could not bear the shame—for months she moaned to herself in self-pity, and swore to have the photo editor's head on a plate. Meriting only an *and friend* in the society pages is the print equivalent of the fashion finger.

Our junk finally docked on the island, and as we disembarked, it was apparent that the Chinese Orphans Society had spared no expense: there were fire-breathing dancers juggling torches, a colorful dragon parade complete with gongs, multiple Chinese fireworks, intricate and elaborate paper lanterns, even Lucy Liu and Lisa Ling. I searched for Stephan but couldn't find him in the crowd. Everyone else was flitting to and fro, excitedly looking for their place cards, while India and I walked reluctantly up to the check-in table to collect our less-than-auspicious seating assignments. But what was this? As we walked closer, we realized that the event organizers were frantically babbling on cell phones instead of politely escorting guests to their seats.

"They've lost the seating chart!" a breathless socialite explained. "It's a madhouse!"

Without the precise instructions of this most essential document, the usual hierarchy of "good" tables had degenerated into a
completely up-for-grabs event. Henry Kissinger found himself
seated next to a man he called "Fluffy." Barbara Walters was next
to Deborah Norville. Jerry Seinfeld and Jessica Sklar were within
chest-butting distance of Shoshanna Lonstein. Henry Kravis was
seated between *two* ex-wives. India reluctantly took a seat next to
RuPaul. I walked around, looking for an empty space, when I heard
a familiar voice call.

"Cat—Cat—over here."

I turned around. It was Stephan. I could place that ambiguously
Continental accent anywhere! He was sitting at a table alone,
looking dapper in a tuxedo and, I made note, custom-made John
Lobb shoes. The Manolo Blahnik for men. Heaven.

"Hi," I said shyly.

"Hi."

"You can sit here if you like," he offered, and I took the seat
beside him. We watched with amusement as junior committee
chairwomen scrambled about, apologizing profusely to wave after
wave of distressed dinner guests who had paid thousands of dollars
for the privilege of sitting next to their chiropractor.

"It's good to see you." I smiled.

"Indeed. You look lovely."

"Galliano," I confessed modestly. It was my usual response to a
compliment. "Nice hair" was usually followed by "Fekkai." "Fabulous makeup" by "Kevyn." "Exquisite forehead" by "Botox." I like to
give credit since I am an authentic person.

Suddenly, there was a tumult as an exasperated event organizer
discovered a badly dressed middle-aged woman stuffing canapés in
her handbag. "You don't beeelong here," the debutante screeched,
digging her talons into the woman's arm and pulling her from the
caviar. "Guards!"

"Excuse me for a second," Stephan said and approached the
scene. "Bunny," he said, speaking to the frazzled publicist. "It's all
right, why not let her stay?" he asked. "She means no harm."

"Stephan, you don't understand," Bunny Teppit-Rightley argued, her voice crackling in frustration. "She doesn't belong here, this is a *private* party."

"Bunny, please, calm down," Stephan said soothingly. "There's more than enough food for everyone here."

"All right. All right," Bunny growled. "You can stay," she said sternly to the meek woman. "But only because my friend here is nice enough to argue your case."

"Why did you do that?" I asked Stephan, when he returned. "She was just a party crasher. A loser."

Stephan shrugged. "Perhaps. But she'd made it this far. It just seems needlessly cruel and snobby and I don't like to be a part of it. Now, more champagne?" he asked, pouring me a glass.

"Please." I nodded.

"Cat!" It was a familiar booming voice—except this time it wasn't muffled by the sound of helicopter blades or transcontinental static. It could only be Brick.

"Hi, darling." I proffered my hand. Brick looked like he always did. Rich. He was losing his hair, and his postcollegiate beer belly had hardened into a tough paunch, but he was handsome enough; men with a bazillion dollars in their account were handsome by any standard. It came from the burnished sheen that could only be the result of being rich enough to buy everything and anybody, or from the thousand dollars' worth of male beauty products. The Slavic supermodel was dangling on his arm, vacuously staring off into space. The last time I saw Brick—God, I couldn't even remember. He had broken up with me via e-mail.

"So—it's good to see you." Brick nodded. He looked at Stephan skeptically.

"Oh, Brick, this is Stephan of Westonia," I said proudly. "Stephan, this is—"

"Brockton Moorehouse Winthrop," Brick interrupted heartily, shaking his hand. "You look familiar!" he boomed.

"No, I don't believe we've met," Stephan answered with a doubtful smile.

"Polo?"

"Excuse me?"

"Didn't we play on a team together once?"

"Ah, actually, I don't play," Stephan said apologetically.

"So, what's new, Brick?" I asked, changing the subject as it had become tedious.

"Busy—busy. As usual." He shrugged. "You'll have to come out to see us this summer. Got a new player on the team. Venezuelan. Incredible to have on a chukker. We're playing Charles."

That would be Prince Charles to you, he wanted to say. Even with his bazillions Brick was always an irrepressible name-dropper. It was always Steven Spielberg this and Michael Eisner that. Not that there's anything wrong with that, of course.

"Anyway, we'd best be going. Good to see you, Cat. Pasha?" The supermodel minced after him, following two steps behind.

"So, you were together, yes?" Stephan asked when Brick had left.

"How did you know?"

"Oh, easy enough," he said dismissively.

"We were engaged for eight years," I admitted. "But that was a long time ago." Actually, only four months, and then I was discarded like last year's Prada mules, but who was counting? "Who can compete with the Tits from Transylvania?" I asked.

"They are stupendous," he agreed, and my confidence faltered at that.

"So why don't you play polo, darling?" I asked coyly. "I thought you grew up in Argentina."

"Yes, I did," he said heartily. "In Buenos Aires. A beautiful city. Have you ever been?"

"No, but I've always wanted to," I replied, hinting broadly.

"Shame. It's a little bit of Paris in South America. Stupendous." Hmmpf.

"But in answer to your question, I used to play polo, but not since this," he said, motioning to his eye patch.

"Can I ask how—?"

"Sailing accident."

"Wow."

"Yes, unfortunately I'm not much of a sailor either."

Interesting! Self-deprecating *and* handsome. We talked a little more, and I attempted to steer the conversation toward Westonia. "It's a little principality, like, um, Monaco," he explained. "Although not as many tourists."

"Is there gambling?" I asked. If so, my mother probably knew it well, I told him.

"No, not really. Not like Monte Carlo. Mostly just a bunch of peasants and their livestock. It's very barren, very rocky. A dreadful place."

"Do you wish you weren't kicked out?" I sighed dreamily.

"Kicked out?"

"Of the country. By the military junta," I said, remembering the information from the website.

"That was a long time ago," he said soberly. "I had not even been born yet. You know, I find this American obsession with titles really quite appalling."

"Oh?"

"Because it's all so meaningless. Why should it make a difference who my great-great-great-grandfather was? It doesn't. Titles are so worthless," he said carelessly.

"For you, maybe," I protested. "But then again, you have one."

He shrugged, and I was suitably impressed by his casual indifference to such a genetic stroke of luck. If I had a title, you could be certain I would have had all of Manhattan bowing so deeply everyone's foreheads would bear footprints.

"So what brought you to New York?" I asked.

"Oh, ah . . . I was . . . transferred."

"By your bank?" I asked, picturing a large investment bank on Wall Street.

"Yes, yes. Right. I'm with Civilian Financial Citation Holdings, but enough about me—my life is boring. What about you?"

"What do you want to know?"

"Whatever you want to tell me," he said, giving me a crooked smile. So I told him. Everything. All about my parents, and Hollywood, and Japan—and he even said he thought he had recognized me, which was a lie but a nice one. I realized I was actually enjoying his company rather than merely pretending to, which was a *nouveau* experience. Usually I found that most successful men tended to bore you with the details of their business, investments, or current fascination with maneuvering their twin-hulled, dual-finned America's Cup catamaran around the globe. Surprisingly, Stephan seemed to be more interested in learning about me than telling me about himself. I made a mental note to tell India that small talk was surprisingly easy—all I had to do was talk about myself. "I don't think I mentioned it the last time we spoke," I said, "but I'm adopting a Chinese baby."

His eyes widened. "Really. I didn't think you were so . . . serious about your commitment to the cause." I knew it! *Floored.*

"Well—you know, I mean, it's just that it's all well and good to throw parties for them and drink champagne on their behalf, but I thought I would make a personal contribution instead," I said modestly.

"I agree. So, when are you going to China?"

"Oh, I'm not," I protested. "I've sent my au pair."

He laughed again—a deep and resonant laugh that was warm and generous, so that I didn't think he was really laughing *at* me. I started laughing as well, because come to think of it, the situation was absurd. I had sent my au pair to China to pick up a baby! What was I thinking? He seemed to like it though.

"Darling, I'm not joking," I said, when our laughter had subsided.

"Oh, I never doubted it."

If he was going to be a handbag, I decided, Stephan would definitely be an Hermès. They kept you on the waiting list forever, but once it's yours, it's irreplaceable. Brick would be more like something you chucked after the trend had passed for small, embroidered shoulder bags in the shape of French pastry that were never big enough to hold all your essentials.

"Stephan! Stephan!" This time we were interrupted by Cece Phipps-Langley, the socialite who had told me all about him in the first place. She sped toward our table like a heat-seeking missile in duchesse satin and antique Victorian jewelry. "Oh, hi, Cat," she said in a less-than-enthusiastic tone. "Did you see Brick and Pasha? Such a doll, isn't she just?"

"Just," I replied, curling my lip.

"Stephan, darling, you can't sit all by yourself here in the dark. There are people I want you to meet," she said, grasping his arm protectively. "You don't mind, do you, Cat?" she asked.

"No, of course not."

"Excuse me," Stephan said reluctantly. "It's good to see you again. Good luck with the baby."

"Baby!" Cece exclaimed with a contemptuous snort. "Cat doesn't even have a boyfriend!" She gave Stephan a look. "Teeny's over there and she wanted to know where you had wandered off to," she chided, pulling his arm like an impatient helmet-headed Chihuahua.

"It was great to see you again," he said graciously before leaving. "You know," he added, looking thoughtful, "I know somebody who is very much interested in adopting a Chinese baby as well. Would you mind if I—"

"Not at all," I said smoothly, reaching into my vintage Whiting & Davis bag and handing him my card. "I'd be happy to tell them everything I know."

Cece watched with narrowed eyes as he pocketed it.

When they left, I found India by the bar. "This suckths," she said, slurring her words.

"Why, what's wrong?"

India waved her empty flute toward the dance floor, where I spotted her generous patron, the wealthy trannie chaser who provided her with a Fifth Avenue aerie and kept her in collagen treatments and floor-length chinchilla. He was deep in conversation with Venus de Milosevic, India's biggest rival in the transsexual stakes. Venus was a fierce Serbian drag queen, whose popular cabaret act involved taking no prisoners.

"Why I oughta . . ." India said, lunging drunkenly in their direction.

It took all of my power to restrain her from confronting them.

"Darling, let it go. She's nothing. He's only paying attention to her because lately you've been ignoring him in favor of your nineteen-year-old go-go dancer. He'll come around eventually."

"And the bah's run hout of chumpagne, can you believe it?" She hiccuped.

"Darling, listen to me. I've got great news. Stephan's asked for my number."

India raised her eyebrows. "You don't (hic) say?"

"Well, actually he said it was for a friend. Someone interested in adopting a Chinese baby," I confessed. "I gave him my card. Do you think he'll call?"

"Why (hic) wouldn't he?"

"I don't know. Maybe it really was for a friend," I said morosely, looking wistfully to where Teeny, Cece, and Stephan were sharing a laugh with Brick and Pasha. Teeny was touching Stephan's arm lightly as she giggled at something he said.

"Nonthense," India declared. "Sthe's thill (hic) married to that Austhrian ballet danther."

"That's never stopped her before," I reminded India. "Do you know, I swear there's something different about him tonight."

India shrugged. "I didn't nothithe."

"I did. Is it the hair? Does he seem taller, maybe?"

"Maybe," India conceded. "Or maybe you're juth theeing things (hic). Oh, wait, there is thomething . . ."

Just then the bartender miraculously found an unopened bottle of bubbly and India forgot her train of thought in her determination to score herself a glass.

*   *   *

I returned home to find a message on the machine from the hotel in San Marco. Apparently I had just missed my mother by a few days. Sigh. There would be no emergency funds coming my way, so it looked like I'd have to face the music—or more specifically, my accountant.

7. life beyond cashmere

Mr. Bartleby-Smythe was a nice fellow of florid complexion and meticulous handwriting. He had known me since I was a baby, and could probably say he'd pinched my inner thighs. As Daddy's most trusted adviser and the executor of the will, he had been responsible for my financial well-being ever since I was ten years old. In college, it was he who convinced my father that I would actually use the money to pay for tuition instead of endless shopping sprees. Daddy had been quite sore over the Tokyo debacle—he couldn't understand how an underage model could accumulate so many debts.

Sarah Lawrence was open-minded enough to consider a few years at prep school, several with a Hollywood acting coach, and my stint in Tokyo's school of hard knocks equivalent to a GED and accepted me.

What I learned in college: abnormal behavior, method acting, how to seduce your roommate's boyfriend.

If Hollywood was all about the size of your entourage and Tokyo the quality of your look book, college was all about discovering the social activist within. I threw myself completely into an aristobohemian lifestyle. Like most of my friends, my room smelled of patchouli and I hardly bathed. I ate couscous and organic veggies, took back the night, wrote angry, affected poetry referring cleverly to my genitalia, and attempted to grow dreadlocks. I hosted communist tea parties, organized financial aid sit-ins, staged Columbus Day protests, renounced all material possessions, and debated Wittgenstein's theories while conducting numerous affairs with bearded professors decked out in full *haute* tenure (suede-patch sport coats, scuffed Nubucks).

Except for my inability to keep awake during class, I was the perfect student. Plus, I was special—the only one in school who had a trust fund *and* received financial aid. See, even though I received an exorbitant allowance that should have been more than enough to keep me in J. Crew pea coats in every color, I spent it faster than the bank could deposit it. Thus, the amount was hardly enough to sustain *all* of my activities. Radical chic didn't come cheap, mind you. Someone had to pay for all those placards and megaphones. By the end of the semester I was banned from opening a checking account at the local bank, and evicted from a series of luxury apartments. Through Mr. Bartleby-Smythe, Daddy would always send another check—he was relieved that I was actually still in school. He was so proud when I graduated Phi Beta Kappa, especially since Sarah Lawrence didn't bother with such things as grades.

"Ah, Cat, come in," Mr. Bartleby-Smythe said jovially, ushering me into his mahogany-paneled office. "I haven't seen you in a while. I was starting to wonder if you'd forgotten about us."

"Oh, Mr. B-S." I laughed.

"So," Mr. Bartleby-Smythe said, easing into his club chair. He smiled affably, peering at me over half-moon glasses. "I'm glad you decided to come by. We've been trying to get a hold of you, you know."

"Really?" I asked innocently.

"Yes, but every time we call, someone answers the phone in Spanish. I wasn't sure if we had your correct phone number."

"Mmmm . . . how strange."

"Now, you must have noticed we haven't sent you a check in a while."

I shrugged as if it hadn't been the cause for my chronic insomnia. Timidly I asked, "Is there some sort of problem?"

"Well, there seems to be some trouble with your Citibank accounts."

"Oh, that. Yes, I know. They call me every day. They even wake me up in the morning," I complained. "They want to know why my accounts are overdrawn. Now, I told them I'd talk to you about it. I thought you were taking care of things," I accused him petulantly.

"We *are* taking care of things, my dear. However . . ." Mr. Bartleby-Smythe turned around and opened a file cabinet. He flipped through several folders until he found what he was looking for. "Aha," he said in a satisfied tone. He laid my bank account statements on his desk, several from Citibank and others bearing Cayman Islands or Swiss deposit identification numbers.

"We've been redirecting funds to try to cover your expenses. But . . ."

"But?"

Mr. Bartleby-Smythe sighed heavily. "Cat, I don't know how to tell you this."

"Just give it to me straight," I said, holding my breath.

"All right, then. You're broke. There is absolutely nothing left."

"Excuse me?" A sharp intake of breath. Water! I needed water!

He took a red pen and began circling several large figures—ones with many zeroes after them. "Here is what your twenty-fifth birthday party cost you *this* year."

"But I thought we had a corporate sponsor." I was bewildered.

"For the privilege of attaching their good name to your own—or should I say, Samantha Boardman's and Aerin Lauder's." He looked at me sternly. "You know I don't approve of that sort of misrepresentation. Harrrummph. In any case, Mercedes-Benz paid for transportation to and from the party for the VIP guests. You covered everything else. The cost of flying in 'N Sync from their European tour and back. Rental of the space, the construction of a makeshift concert stage—the liquor bill alone was enough to set you back several months. Then there was the pyrotechnic display, and some kind of special designer candles."

I gagged, remembering I hadn't even been able to blow out the candles myself!

"This is how much your publicist's retainer is costing."

Ouch. That Swiss bitch sure didn't come cheap.

"This is the household payroll." He circled another extravagant sum.

"And this was the amount you spent on clothing and entertainment last week." It was the most colossal number yet. Mr. Bartleby-Smythe grimaced. "Twenty thousand dollars for a ticket to a *charity* ball? You're certainly not in a position to be a philanthropist right now."

I cringed, looking over his notes hurriedly, none of it making any sense. Positively abhorred math. It's not that I couldn't add (except when I couldn't), but math made me irritable and pimply. And my dermatologist was rigorous about my skin. So I never risked a breakout by bothering with such things as bank statements, credit card bills, or the latest on Catherine Zeta-Jones's love life. Such things simply made me ill. And I hated being sick more than I hated math. In fact, I forbade myself to get sick, except when it was absolutely necessary, of course. One should always make allocations for such emergencies. I was nothing if not a woman who believed crises must be placated and seduced away with mud baths, aromatherapy, and Asprey & Garrard. If all that failed, simply throw more money into it and maybe it will go away. Believing myself to be ill when something didn't suit me was another expensive habit. For instance, I never took the subway due to a small, medically prescribed claustrophobic condition—I really had to fight for that one. It behooved me to stay on the cutting edge of all new medical trends—I'd already been diagnosed as passive-aggressive, manic-depressive, anorexic, bulimic, alcoholic, and an overeater suffering from affective seasonal disorder, social anxiety disorder, and low self-esteem.

"I don't care! Listen, there's got to be some money left somewhere, correct? I just can't be broke! I need money for something incredibly important!" I raged. Bannerjee had called the other day from Shanghai with horrifying news. Apparently illegal Chinese baby brokers didn't take Amex. I was incensed, as Heidi and I had already planned a "Welcome Home Mei-Mei" party at the "21" Club to properly welcome my new Chinese child to New York. Heidi's office had been working on the guest list for days, celebrities who were sure to be sympathetic to the plight of Chinese orphans. Susan Sarandon and Tim Robbins. Richard Gere. Irina Pantaeva. Everyone on the Chinese Orphans Benefit Committee. Even Stephan was sure to attend. I promised Bannerjee I'd come up with the money somehow.

"I'll arrange it immediately," I told her. "But remember, once you have the baby, make sure she doesn't eat any more of that greasy Chinese food! I want her on organic milk!"

Mr. Bartleby-Smythe had never let me down before. "There has just got to be a way," I wheedled.

"Well, Citibank is willing to settle your accounts, and you have just enough in your last Swiss bank account to cover it. It's a desperate measure, but there's nothing that can be done. I suggest you begin to make some changes in your life."

"How could Daddy do this to me?" I moaned. "I thought he said he would make sure I would be taken care of for the rest of my life."

"Your father left you quite a legacy. And your broker invests well, but you've displayed an uncanny ability to spend any profits made before the market closes."

"So that's it? I'm poor?" I could not believe the words coming out of my mouth: *I'm* and *poor* did not an acceptable sentence make.

"Upper class and sinking fast," this nasty little man responded.

This was a sobering situation indeed. I had to keep myself afloat long enough to stay in Stephan's social circle, otherwise how would I ever position myself as his betrothed? But the thought of living less than large was less than appealing. Would I have to eat government cheese? Would I have to learn a "skill"? Was I going to be just another statistic in the welfare roll?

"This is terrible, terrible!" I moaned. Please God, I prayed, just let me get through this and I'll never buy three-thousand-dollar gem-encrusted marabou-feather Gucci jeans again. Or order baby girls from China just to impress a potential suitor.

"What am I supposed to do?" I wailed. "I'm about to become a mother."

"You don't say?" He peered at me over his desk. "I don't know how you do it, Cat, but you always look so slim. I suppose the father isn't of any help?" he asked sternly.

"No—no, there is no father!" I announced dramatically.

"Well, there is a way. But it would require an immense sacrifice on your part."

"Anything! Anything!" I promised feverishly.

"Give up the penthouse triplex. We could put it on the market; it's a great time for sellers right now, and my office has fielded inquiries as to your willingness to sell the place."

"Never. I'm not selling." I shook my head furiously. Give up the glass-enclosed, Art Deco penthouse? Over my dead—

"The mortgage is killing you. I suggest you lease it and stay at a less expensive place while trying to get back on your feet."

"But—but—where would I go?" I whined.

Mr. Bartleby-Smythe ignored me and continued his lecture. "However, simply moving won't be enough. I suggest you begin to cut corners while we explore your financial possibilities. For now, why not opt for lamb's wool instead of cashmere. Buy generic instead of organic. Max Factor instead of Maximillian Furs."

Mr. Bartleby-Smythe shook his head. "Cat, you're already twent-ni—"

"Five. Twenty-five," I snapped.

"All right. Twenty-five years old," he agreed, with raised eyebrows. "The point is, you've got a long way ahead of you, so you must try to live within your means before things get too dire. I'm serious, Cat. This is it. You do realize your mother has never been much help."

I nodded sadly. Poor Mummy. More often than not, she was usually in just as much financial trouble as I was—when I was younger Daddy explained the reason we never had her phone number in Europe was because she was constantly on the move from her creditors. Hmm . . . that was an idea. After all, if I listened to what Mr. Bartleby-Smythe was saying, I'd have to trade in my double-Gs for BCBG, and the sable for something synthetic.

"Have you ever considered . . ."

A lost Swiss bank account? The lottery?

". . . a job?" he finished.

I reeled, clutching my forehead in despair. Actually *work* for money? Oh, the humanity!

8. three plans and an unexpected coincidence

Life on a budget was worse than could be imagined—my nails were horribly chipped and *pas de massage* for days. I'd even been re-potty trained as I couldn't afford colonics anymore and had been forced to use the regular "toilet." To acclimate to my new low-profile lifestyle, I enrolled in survival tactics at the Learning Annex: Advanced Fast Food, and Public Transportation: Beyond the Madison Avenue Bus. Exhausting. But there was no way I was going to give up my zip code without a fight, especially since there was Bannerjee and the baby to think about.

As it turned out, giving Bannerjee the Amex was doubly worthless—it couldn't buy an illegal baby, nor did it solve her "visa" problem. She finally explained that she didn't need the kind of Visa that bought Jimmy Choo shoes but the kind they give out at U.S. embassies. I wasn't aware there was *another* kind. So not only did I need to come up with enough cash to buy the baby, but I would also need to conjure up this so-called visa to get her out of China as well.

With those things in mind, I busied myself by making a list of potential moneymaking scams, I mean, *schemes* to extricate myself from the horrid financial K-hole I had fallen into:

1. *Estate Sale*—Has potential, although possibility of anyone buying last season's fashions slim. Have placed call to Tiffany Dubin, the fashion curator, about my mother lode of Gucci embroidered mules and python-print dresses.

2. *Declare Self Messiah*—Helpful India pointed out religions don't have to pay taxes and can mandate donations at will. Have placed call to John Travolta's PR manager and ordered a copy of *Dianetics*.

3. *Launch E-VIParty.com*—Decided to sell my party invitations on a website where ordinary Joes can bid for the right to attend Manhattan's most exclusive events. This week's offerings include a funeral for a highly esteemed fashion editor, a baby shower for a pregnant socialite, and the launch of Geraldo Rivera's new magazine, G.

Boo. None of my ideas panned out as planned. Tiffany's people called to say my collection of millennial Gucci was a no-go. Apparently I would have to wait more than a few years before these were declared "classic." Nor would I be able to declare myself the Messiah, as an Orthodox rabbi from Crown Heights had already done so. And while E-VIParty.com was doing a brisk business, I soon received nasty phone calls from several annoyed publicists, including my own. Apparently they were receiving phone calls from a Camaro-load of no-names from New Jersey for their events, and when these arrivistes were asked how the private RSVP numbers had been infiltrated, all signs pointed back to my website. "Caf, I simfly von't allow vis. Ees bad for imaje," Heidi snarled, when I explained what happened. Reluctantly, I sent home my heartbroken staff of twelve-year-old computer geeks, who monitored the party invitation auction website for a salary of beer, pizza, and pornography.

I was so depressed I cabbed to Barneys and charged new platform pumps to my MasterCard pronto. So much for that nonshopping embargo.

Of course, there was still the off chance that Stephan of Westonia would fall head over heels in love with me, acquiesce to a quickie marriage, and elevate me back to the upper echelon, where I belonged, thereby resolving all my financial difficulties. But it had already been two weeks and I had yet to hear from him, or this so-called "friend" who was interested in Chinese adoption. Against my better nature, I had taken to waiting religiously by the phone in the hope that it would ring.

"Has he called yet?" India asked a few days after E-VIParty.com was shelved.

"No," I moped. "Maybe he's not interested."

"How could he not be interested in you!" India said, offended at the very thought. "Of course not. He's probably just busy. Why didn't you ask for his number?"

"Because," I whined, "I would never call him anyway."

"Why not?"

India was of the mind that all the incredibly silly traditions of modern dating were just that—incredibly silly. If India wanted a man, she stepped right up and told him, point-blank. It usually worked or else the gentleman in question called the police. The sight of a six-foot-four transsexual in five-inch heels and full-throttle seductive mode was more than ordinary men could handle. Fortunately for India, she was attracted to sterner stuff: garbage men, nineteen-year-old go-go dancers, construction workers, and all sorts of "rough trade." But even India wasn't invincible. Since the night of the Chinese Orphans Benefit, her generous patron had been incommunicado and, worse, had been spotted at the transgender watering-hole Edelweiss, in none other than Venus de Milosevic's clutches. Not an ideal situation, especially since India's rent was due in a week.

* * *

Although they were tempting, I purposefully avoided several charity galas where I was sure to bump into Stephan. For one, I didn't have the money to spare for a ticket, and it would just be too embarrassing to see him in public while he hadn't called me in the interim.

It was pure luck that I brushed past him as I left India's building one evening. Wearing a dapper three-button herringbone-tweed suit and carrying a smart attaché case, Stephan crossed the street in front of me just as I was hailing a taxicab.

"Cat!"

"Stephan!"

"I'm so glad I ran into you!" he said without a trace of insincerity.

"Really?"

"I've been meaning to tell you—my friends decided not to adopt."

"No?"

"At least not from China. They went Romanian. They saw a Very Special Episode of 20/20."

"Oh, how wonderful," I said, wondering if they knew something I didn't. Was Romanian more trendy than Chinese?

"I've been meaning to call you and I know you won't believe it, but I lost your number. I put it in my coat pocket and it must have fallen out," he explained.

"You did?"

"You're very hard to track down, you know. I called Information but you aren't listed. I asked Cece if she had your number and she said her maid lost her Rolodex. Then I was sure I'd see you at the Fiesta for Fetal Disease, but you weren't even at the opening at the Brecht revival at the Prada store downtown."

"I've been . . . uh . . . away," I said, extremely pleased that he had noticed my absence.

"So how is she?"

"Who?"

"Your baby."

"My baby? Oh, right. Her arrival has been delayed . . . er . . . indefinitely." I felt a strong wave of guilt. Bannerjee had called the other night, complaining about being stuck in a dingy hotel room watching MTV China (Lionel Ritchie videos on constant airplay). She told me she didn't move all the way from Sri Lanka to the Upper East Side only to be stuck in a flea trap in Shanghai. I had meant to send an application for Banny's visa to the U.S. embassy, but India told me it would be much, much easier if I turned to an immigration lawyer on Fulton Street instead.

"Oh, that's too bad."

"I know," I agreed mournfully. I was never one for delayed gratification, and reading *What to Expect When You're Expecting from China*, as well as *Dr. Spock's International Adopted Baby Book* only made the baby's absence more pronounced. To think that I was losing precious bonding moments every second she spent in that awful orphanage!

"Anyway, what are you doing here?" I asked.

"I live up the block," he replied, and waved toward a high-rise farther up Fifth Avenue.

"Oh, so you've finally settled on an apartment?" I asked, remembering the Corcoran brokers Cece had mentioned.

"You could say that." He nodded.

"I'm just around the corner, at 740½ Park. The penthouse." My co-op was *right next door* to 740 Park, the most prestigious address in Manhattan, the palatial building which the Lauders, the Rosses, the Steinbergs all called home at one point, and where John D. Rockefeller once owned his famous penthouse triplex. Unfortunately, Daddy had been rejected by the 740 co-op board, and had had to settle for 740½.

"Excellent."

"We're practically neighbors," I said. "Do you want a ride home?" I asked, as a taxi pulled up by the curb.

"No—no." He shook his head. "I like to walk."

"You walk?"

"I walk everywhere. It's a great way to see the city. . . . Hey, maybe . . . oh, forget it."

"What?"

"No, you probably won't want to."

"Want to what?"

"Would you like to take a walk with me?"

"Right now?" I asked.

"Sure, why not?" He smiled.

"Walk?" I repeated, looking down at my Manolos skeptically. "I suppose I could try," I conceded, although I preferred my views of the city to be through tinted-glass windows. I sent the cab away.

"C'mon. There's something I want to show you. I think you'd enjoy it." I took the arm he offered and we ventured into the twilight.

It was almost midnight when I arrived home. The neighborhood was deserted save for random bunches of sixteen-year-old Spence girls breaking curfew, wearing skimpy dresses and their mother's Gucci heels on their way downtown to Spa.

"I had a fabulous time," I told him, and giggled as I looked down at my feet. Instead of my caramel slingbacks was a pair of canvas Tweety Bird sneakers purchased at a ninety-nine-cent store. I had lasted all of ten blocks in my high heels—a veritable record.

"So did I." He smiled.

"You know," I said shyly. "There's a new restaurant that's just opened around here."

"There is?"

"Yes . . ." I said, and held my breath. "Maybe we can check it out sometime. You know, if you're not, um, busy or anything."

He shrugged. "Why not? Maybe I'll stop by sometime next week and we'll do that."

"Anytime," I said. "You know where I live. Come by and see me."

"I will."

We stood there awkwardly, and it struck me that I didn't know what to do next. I was so out of practice! He stood with his hands behind his back and looked at me expectantly.

"Well . . . good night," I ventured.

"Good night," he said, and continued to stand there, away from me.

I gave him a half-smile and turned away. The night doorman held open the door expectantly and I walked through it. Oh, well. Next time.

9. *the new tenant*

The next day I realized that if I wanted to continue to eat I would have to exchange gift certificates I'd received as birthday presents for cash. Barring no other options, I placed a call to Mr. Bartleby-Smythe.

"I'm willing to lease the penthouse," I told him reluctantly.

"Wonderful news!" he replied. "And it just so happens I've already got a tenant for the apartment. I'll send them over immediately."

Since I would have to let go of the household staff, I temporarily settled that issue by deciding to move into a one-bedroom suite at the Mercer Hotel in SoHo. Hotel living would more than make up for the loss of my chef, my butler, my footman, the army of liveried servants, and the woman who came in every week to alphabetize my moisturizers. My belongings were going into storage, and were neatly packed into an array of T. Anthony steamer trunks. It never ceased to amaze me how much stuff I've accumulated over the years: Greek and Roman statuary from my antiquing phase, the many canvases of broken crockery, not to mention my collection of ancient Japanese kimonos from the fifteenth century. Packing away my clothes posed a Herculean task and I sorely missed Bannerjee's adept sense of organization, but for now vintage, designer, vintage designer, ironic, costume, evening, and hip-hop were all scrambled together in one big loading case and I figured I could sort it all out later when she returned.

I was taking care of last-minute errands, making sure I had remembered to pack all the unopened bottles of champagne from the Sub-Zero, wrapping my Lejaby bras in acid-free tissue paper, when India popped in from the other room. She was helping me move, as well as helping herself to some of my possessions. Her financial situation was just as desperate as mine, and I marveled that she could be so nonplussed concerning the about-turn her generous patron's heart had taken. The possibility of eviction didn't seem to upset her as much as it should have. "Oh, I'm not worried, darling," she said. "After all, I can always move in with you at the Mercer." Which was true, although if Bannerjee ever came back with the baby it would make for cramped quarters indeed. What with India's wigs and my shoes, there would be no space for a cradle, let alone the gargantuan Chanel baby stroller I had set my heart on for the arrival of my first-bought.

"Cat, you don't need this, do you?" India asked, holding up two glowsticks from my rave phase. "I think I can put them to use. . . ."

I was about to protest when the doorman buzzed.

"A visitor for Miss McAllister," he announced on the intercom.

"Who's there?" India inquired.

"I've no idea." I shrugged. What did this look like, a Southern porch? True New Yorkers know *never* to arrive unannounced.

The butler opened the door, and before I could see who it was, a piercing sound assaulted my eardrums. "CAAATTT darling!!" There was only one woman in Manhattan whose voice decibel range matched my own. It could only be . . .

"Teeny?" I gasped.

"I'm, uh—" She was interrupted by muscle-bound movers who elbowed her out of the way, gingerly lifting Marlene Dietrich's grand piano (I still hadn't met a dead-celebrity auction I could resist). A harried-looking man followed her inside. He wiped his brow profusely and surveyed the premises with a proprietary air I didn't much care for.

"What are you doing here?" I asked Teeny suspiciously. "And who, pray tell, are you?" I gave the skittish fellow an icy glance.

"Mr. Finn's the name," he said, offering his hand.

Teeny ignored my question and bent down to proffer me a powdered cheek, which I pecked out of habit. Was that *my* perfume she was wearing? "India darling," she said, turning to India.

"Hello," India greeted coolly, with a modicum of courtesy.

"What are you doing here?" I repeated sharply.

Teeny surveyed the empty penthouse, ran her fingers over the mantel, examined the nonexistent dust on her fingertips, and answered innocently. "Oh, didn't you know? My divorce from Dashiell isn't complete yet, but I've already left him. And I've always loved this old place. Cat, your mother had exquisite taste." Teeny tapped her kitten heels on the marble floor. "I never thought it would be on the market," she marveled.

"Oh, undoubtedly, we've had our eye on it for a while," Mr. Finn agreed.

"Excuse me—?" I choked.

I suddenly remembered Mr. Bartleby-Smythe's eagerness to rid me of my penthouse. "I know someone who would be very interested in your apartment," he had leered. If only I had known he had meant Teeny! How could he? To think I had trusted him with my trust fund!

"Mr. Bartleby-Smythe sent you?" I asked.

"Yes, indeedy. Called us right away, and hi-ho, off we went."

"But I'm not ready—I thought I still had until next week," I protested.

"Oh no, oh no. I'm sorry, madam. No, the lease has been signed, and as your broker, I can assure you all the papers are in order. You can ask Mr. Bartleby-Smythe, and he'll confirm that it's all been arranged. Mrs. Van der Hominie—"

"Lady Van der Hominie," Teeny corrected.

"Lady Van der Hominie now has possession of this apartment."

"But this is only a temporary move; I'm only leasing it for now," I snapped.

"For sure, for sure." Mr. Finn nodded, but I caught him giving Teeny a smug, knowing look.

"I think I'll have a look around," Teeny said. "I just want to make sure everything is as it should be." Without bothering to wait for a reply, she began a room-by-room investigation of the family homestead, her heels scratching the beautiful travertine floor.

"Perhaps we should be going," I conceded, sighing.

"Cat—no!" India argued. "It's so . . ."

Utterly humiliating. But thankfully, India didn't rub salt on the wound.

"Darling, it's all right, I'm fine," I assured her. "The moving men have finished clearing out my boxes and there doesn't seem to be much use in carrying on this conversation anymore."

"Oh, Cat!" India cried, and forcefully hugged me to her bountiful chest. "Don't worry, darling. I know you'll be back here in no time." We huddled in the doorway of the apartment that was no longer mine. Teeny followed us out.

"Ta-ta, darlings. Oh, by the way, I'm having a petit dinner party to celebrate my new home. I'd love to have all of you here. You too, India," she said. "Next week, *oui?*"

"I'm busy," India said bluntly.

"I'm, ah . . . getting my hair done," I said, lying badly.

"Well, let me know, dears. Or better yet, stop by. After all, you know where I live." Teeny gave me a wicked smile.

India and I were inside the elevator when a bloodcurdling scream erupted from inside the apartment.

"AAAARRRRGGGHHHH!!" There was a galloping of heels on the floor, and suddenly a red-faced Teeny was in front of us, holding back the elevator doors with her bare hands.

"BITCH!" Teeny spat. "Where is the closet! You know it's the only reason I wanted this apartment!" Mummy's custom-built, temperature-controlled closet, my one true inheritance, was now relocated to a storage locker in Midtown while I assessed my real estate possibilities. A huge, ugly, double-height hole in the wall was all that remained of this marvel.

"Ta-ta, Teeny!" I smiled, wagging my fingers. "Do call. Don't be a stranger."

10. a room with a view

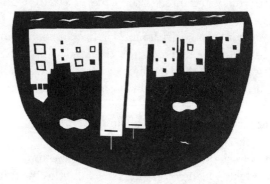

The Mercer Hotel turned out to be an excellent choice. I was in great company—Calvin Klein was a neighbor and I occasionally bumped into Leonardo diCaprio en route to the ice machine. But in the confusion and trauma that accompanied the move, I realized Stephan wouldn't be able to reach me at my old number! I panicked, as I didn't have a clue as to how to get in touch with him without skulking in front of India's building at dusk.

I hadn't seen him since the memorable night we had taken that long walk up Fifth Avenue. We had walked until Fifth Avenue really wasn't Fifth Avenue anymore—when the buildings no longer had white-gloved doormen but instead had bums hanging out in front of their vestibules.

"What are we doing here?" I had asked him, looking around fearfully.

"I said I wanted to show you something, didn't I?"

"Yes."

He unlocked the front door to a shabby tenement building on Fifth Avenue and 110th. I had no choice but to follow him inside.

Dear God, it was worse than I had imagined. The hallway was yellow, musty, and fearfully stained. There were cobwebs everywhere, and something smelled powerfully rank.

"This is what you wanted to show me?" I asked. "Darling, I know how the other half lives. I've watched PBS."

"No, no, don't worry. Trust me." He beckoned, holding open the door to an old-fashioned elevator, the kind with a swinging door and that was smaller than my shoe closet. I had to stand quite close to Stephan, which I didn't mind at all. He pressed the top-floor button.

"Darling, really, what is this all about?"

"You'll see."

There was another horrid hallway on the top floor, this one painted a sickly green color, but thankfully the smell from downstairs had faded somewhat. It was quiet, except for the sound of televisions from the other apartments: *I'll take Whoopi for the block.*

"Here we are." He smiled, unlocking a corner apartment.

The first thing I noticed was that it was incredibly dark inside the room. The windows had been boarded up with thick black plastic sheets taped to the glass.

"What's going on here?" I asked fearfully. "Why don't you turn on the light?" It struck me that I didn't know anything about him! Even if he was the Prince of Westonia, what on earth was I doing in a pitch-black tenement apartment?

Stephan closed the door behind him. "Turn around," he said.

"Oh!" I was at a loss for words. "Oh, it's beautiful."

When Stephan had closed the door into the hallway, an image came into focus on the apartment's back wall. A breathtaking view of New York, except that the city was completely upside down and backward. The Empire State Building. The Metropolitan Museum of Art. Central Park. Glorious and wonderful and lovely, at once familiar and strange, given the topsy-turvy angle.

"But how?"

"It's called camera obscura. It's a hobby of mine," he explained.

"You know how a camera is basically a black box with a small pin-hole of light? Well, I've turned this apartment into a black box. A camera. See that small hole of light up there? It reflects the view of New York on the back wall. Like a movie projector, but a real one."

"It's . . . it's . . . amazing."

"I wanted you to see this before it got too dark. Fortunately, the sun is still high and there's enough light to make the projection."

"Wow. But why here?"

"Upper Fifth Avenue has the best views of Manhattan. You can see the entire city from here. It feels right, somehow—the whole city literally turned over on its head. It reminds me that things don't have to be the way they are. That sometimes, it's better to look at things a little differently."

"So this is your . . . studio?" It was obviously just his work space.

"You could call it that," he acknowledged. He switched on the light and the view of New York disappeared.

On closer inspection I noticed that what I thought was black plastic sheets taped to the windowpanes was actually heavy black wool fabric. Unlike the hallway, the apartment was clean and bright. There was nothing in it but a camera on a tripod and a mattress on the floor.

"I didn't know you had a bohemian side," I teased.

"Here, look at this," he said, bringing over a portfolio. The photographs were of the same upside-down view, except at different hours of the day. The most striking one had Stephan in front of it. He was standing right-side up; it was Manhattan that was upside down.

"Thank you for taking me here," I said.

"You're welcome."

◊

But how to let Stephan know that I had moved? I hadn't noticed a phone in his studio, so that was out. Then I remembered his website, which was sure to have the name of his PR agent, at least. I logged onto Stephan-of-Westonia.com, and the computer screen flashed, "Domain name available! Register Stephan-of-Westonia dot com today!" *Quel étrange.* I called Cece Phipps-Langley as a last resort to ask her if she had his information.

"Oh, Cat . . . Stephan's new phone number? I actually don't have it. He was staying here for a while, but I don't know where he is now."

"Yes, I know he's not there anymore," I said impatiently.

"Yes. While he was looking around for a place. But he's gone now. For the life of me, I simply can't remember."

"Do you know if he has a phone in his studio?"

"What studio?"

"Oh, never mind." Stephan seemed like a private person and probably would not have shared his hobby with Cece.

"What about his work number? Do you have that?"

"No. I'm sorry. My personal assistant just left and the new girl hasn't sorted my Rolodex yet. My life is in absolute tatters."

"Would you know where he works?"

"Something like the Civilians Group? Civilized Bank? Civilization Finance? CCGG? CDGW? I can't keep track. Something like that."

There were no listings for any of the above, although I did find a Citation Group Finance Holdings, which seemed close enough. I dialed the number, but they didn't have a listing for Stephan of Westonia.

"Stephan Owestoya, did you say?"

"No, *of Westonia,*" I corrected.

"Of Westonia?" the receptionist asked doubtfully.

"Yes. It's a . . . title."

"A title? What kind? Vice president?"

"I don't know."

"His last name isn't Owestoya?"

"No. He doesn't have a last name."

"I'm sorry, ma'am, but if he doesn't have a last name, I can't track him down for you."

It was no use. If I called my old apartment and asked Teeny to give him a message, it would be practically an invitation for her to wreck the relationship before it even began.

"Cat, please come *inside* the building. You're too old to hang around the sidewalk," India beseeched. "This is a nice neighborhood. Think of my property values!"

"You live in a sublet!" I huffed. "But I'm telling you, he lives right down the block. . . ." I argued feebly, pointing off to the distance, where I was sure he resided in palatial, thirty-four-room glory. Somehow the thought of trying to visit him at the camera obscura apartment never entered my mind. As much as I wanted to see him, I wasn't about to venture into Harlem on my own.

fashion weak

11. condé not

Since I had no choice but to actually work for money, I decided I might as well start at the top—at the publications that cataloged the near and dear to my heart: haute couture, starlets, and the proper way to carry one's handbag (scrunched under your arm or tipped at a ninety-degree angle). I would settle for nothing less than a position at *Vogue, Harper's Bazaar, Elle,* or *W.*

Since I've never owned clothes for "work" I decided it was important to find the perfect interview outfit and asked India to accompany me to Barneys, where they still accepted my charge card. I chose an exquisite, fur-trimmed Fendi black-leather jumpsuit, which zipped up snug and tight.

"Professional diva!" I crowed.

"Boardroom bitch!" India agreed.

"*Couture* Fridays!"

"Condé *Nasty!*" India decreed, which of course, was the highest compliment of all.

The Condé Nast offices are located in a shiny new silver building in Times Square, whose construction had resulted in one very minor death. I marveled at the wave after wave of bare-legged editors who wafted into the building wearing clothes more suited to a weekend in St. Thomas than Midtown Manhattan, and remembered India once telling me that it was like this all the time—even in the middle of winter, in zero-degree weather. "Which only proves that I'm right. Fashion is *beyond* the weather," India had said. I took the famous Condé Nast elevators and prepared myself for the infamous elevator stare-down between competing editrixes, but only found myself next to a slovenly maintenance man. I gave him a hard glare nevertheless. Overalls are so *over*.

Once at Human Resources, I entertained myself by guessing which magazine each applicant was there for. The high-cheekboned wench in the deconstructed sweater with an unfinished hem? Definitely *Vogue*. The bubbly girl in dark-rinse jeans? She had to be *Mademoiselle* material. Cousin It in the corner, chewing her hair? She was no parts Condéscending or nasty. What on earth was she going for? Mail room, I decided. I was kept waiting for an infinite period of time, and resorted to bribing the receptionist with the contents of my Birkin bag (two invitations to a movie screening, and my discount card at Bliss Spa) in order to convince her to add my interview to the recruitment director's schedule.

"Cat McAllister?" A peroxide blonde in a trim pair of leather pants and vertiginous high heels asked as she walked into the reception area.

"Yes!" I replied, practically bouncing off the chair. I was so glad! The sooner I got the interview over with, the sooner I could get out of my Fendi straitjacket—I mean jumpsuit.

"Hi. I'm Lark Hodgson. Editorial manager of Condé Nast. Fabulous outfit," she observed, and I felt vindicated. She gazed at me keenly. "You look familiar . . . don't I know you from somewhere?"

"I was a bit of a child actress in my youth," I allowed modestly. "Maybe you remember it? A dramatic comedy about an orphan adopted by an interracial couple?"

"Nope, don't think so." Lark shrugged. "Hey, weren't you at Barneys not too long ago? Returning a bundle of clothes? And your friend kept pulling this box of shoes from your hands and finally you wrestled her to the floor? As I remember it was quite a scene."

"Oh, no, I don't think so." I blushed.

"Anyway, come on in," she said. I followed her into a corner office that boasted a vast and sterile emptiness except for a perfectly squat 1920s Bauhaus-style Charlotte Periand black leather and chrome couch. A profusion of flowers backlit by a spotlight along the ledge that gave the office the air of an exquisitely prestigious funeral home. Black-and-white photographs on her desk displayed a curly-haired husband and two adorable blond children.

"What can I do for you, Cat?" she asked politely. "I've read your résumé, and I'm not quite sure what to make of it. What exactly brings you here?"

"I'm here for a position at *Vogue*. You are hiring, aren't you?"

"Well—yes," she hedged.

"Great! When do I start?" I asked eagerly. "I'm available immediately. And I'd love an office like this one if there are any left."

"Oh, no, no, no." Lark laughed, wiping tears from her face. "Where did you get that idea? You'd have to start as a fashion assistant."

"Start as an *assistant*?" I blanched.

"Junior market editor. Basically, steam-cleaning clothes and making sure the models don't eat during shoots. There are several, you know, who are just *addicted* to chocolate. We really have to save them from themselves. You'll have to monitor them very carefully."

"But junior market editor? That doesn't sound right. Don't they make twenty-three thousand dollars a year?"

"Yes," she answered matter-of-factly, as if that wouldn't be some sort of problem.

"Darling, I was thinking something along the lines of contributing-editor-at-large," I said in my most confident tone. "You know, a fat little contract. A mortgage. Something like that." Several of

New York's most high-profile socialites held exalted and lucrative positions at the magazine; I thought it was only right that I be asked to join their ranks as well.

She laughed lightly. "Oh, no. You've no experience, and we're not looking for freeload—I mean, freelancers."

"But—twenty-three thousand dollars a year?"

"Sweetie, you *do* have a trust fund, don't you?" she inquired, as if the very idea that I would not have one was a subject of utmost hilarity. Didn't she know even trust funds ran out? And as for royalty checks from rerun episodes of my one canceled sitcom, which neither TV Land nor Lifetime wanted (although it did prove quite popular in the Philippines and former Soviet republics)—these residuals netted me a fat $5 a month. So at $23,000 a year, I'd be making less than India's armpit waxer.

"It's yours if you want it. So, it's agreed then? Twenty-three thousand dollars a year, plus benefits, which includes medical and dental and plastic."

"Plastic?"

"Surgery—but only one lipo a year. You're expected to keep your end up. Weigh-in is nine sharp every morning. And silly me, I almost forgot—there is one last thing," she said, whipping out a strange contraption that looked like a flashlight with an LCD display. "It's a fat analyzer," Lark explained. "Don't worry, we had models in the office who were ninety-nine pounds and twenty-four percent fat." She chuckled. She pointed it toward my arm and read the results.

"You're forty-seven percent fat," she reported matter-of-factly, putting it away with a slightly perturbed look on her face.

How could that be? I never ate anything and adhered to a strict SSV diet—smoke, starve, and vomit, that is.

"It's a little high, especially for us," she said awkwardly. She looked at me skeptically for a moment, then grinned. "But what the hell! Everyone starts out *immense*! And we desperately need someone to organize the fashion closet. It's a complete nightmare right now. *Vogue* hosted a charity benefit last weekend and, well," she giggled to herself, "the staff attacked the racks! You'll have to track down the eighteen-karat Chanel dress—I'm not sure who took off with it."

Organize the fashion closet? *Please.* I had no choice but to pass on the position. After all, organizing closets was what I had hired my au pair to do. I suddenly missed Bannerjee keenly. She had made my life so easy and carefree. But now she was stuck in China while I tried to come up with enough money to bring her and the baby home.

"I'm sorry, but I don't think I can accept," I demurred politely.

"Really?" Lark asked, her face falling. "We really do need someone to start immediately. Miguel Adrover's new collection is bound to arrive any day now and we desperately need someone to keep an eye on it. You did say you were available, didn't you?"

"I'll think about it," I lied.

"All right, up to you, but between you and me, I've got to tell you these jobs don't last long," she warned, pointing to a fat stack of résumés piled two feet high on her desk. "I know hundreds of girls who would kill to be in your shoes right now." I nodded, but then, I was wearing five-hundred-dollar Dolce & Gabbana sandals, so that was true enough.

Lark and I exchanged limp double-cheek air kisses, and I promised I would let her know soon. I walked out of the silver offices of the Condé Nast building feeling very blue indeed. I was so discouraged I didn't even have the heart to scam an interview at *W, Elle,* or *Harper's Bazaar.* What was I going to do? I had sent Mummy several incredibly urgent cablegrams, but had yet to receive any word. And without a job, I wouldn't have enough money to pay for the baby. No baby, no Stephan. I could tell he was drawn to me because of my magnanimous gesture. "You're not like the other girls, are you, Cat McAllister?" he'd said.

My car and driver pulled up to the curb when I heard what was now a familiar screech from the limousine ahead.

"Cat! Cat! Over here!"

I walked over to the sound. "Teeny?"

She rolled down the tinted windows of her *stretch* limousine. (Shudder—but at least it wasn't white.) "I thought that was you! What were you doing at *Vogue*?"

"Oh, nothing important," I said, feigning casualness. "I'm just incredibly bored all day and I thought, ha-ha, why not try to see if I could help them out at the magazine."

Teeny cocked an eyebrow. "Really?" she asked. "They're great— I love the magazine to death, of course, but they never feature any of our clothes. I just don't understand," she sniped. "I mean, everyone *wears* Tart Tarteen; why I've got all the important Hollywood stylists in and out of our showroom every day."

She pulled me closer to whisper. "You know, Cat, I was thinking . . . you should come work for my company. I'm looking for a spokesmodel. I'll pay you a good salary. Better than Condé Nast, even. What are they offering you? Five hundred thousand dollars for a contributing editor's position? Full mortgage? Town house? Hamptons beach?"

"Really?" I asked, the possibility of all that lovely money blinding me to the fact that this was *Teeny* we were talking about.

Teeny nodded vigorously. "You'll do mall openings, television commercials, conventions . . ."

Conventions? Mall openings? I slowly sank back down to earth.

Teeny smirked when she saw the look on my face. "Well, think about it, would you?"

"Oh, Teeny?" I asked, before she rolled up her window.

"Yes?" she asked, eyes wide.

"I was just wondering if you've received any calls for me. At the apartment, I mean."

"For you?" she repeated thoughtfully, her smile faltering. "I could ask the maids, but no, I don't think so. You did tell everyone you had moved?"

"Yes." I sighed. "Everyone."

With a heavier heart than before, I rang India on my way back to the hotel.

"So how did it go?"

"Terrible. I'm forty-seven percent fat."

"What?"

"They offered me a job as a fashion assistant!"

"Yuck."

"And while I was leaving, I bumped into Teeny. And can you imagine? She offered me a job!"

"The *nerve*," India spat. "To do what?"

"You really don't want to know."

"I can only imagine."

"And I asked her if she had received any calls for me and she said she hadn't."

"She's lying. But don't worry, darling, you'll bump into him soon enough and you can explain everything."

"What about your Mr. Moneybags? Given any thought toward blackmail?"

"I have, but I just don't have it in me. After all, I'm still a *lady*. And if he prefers Venus de Milosevic over me, he can have that two-bit skank."

"Sweetie, I'm at my wits' end here. If I don't find a job quickly—a good one—I don't know what I'll do. I'm a week away from being homeless—I just got my hotel bill. Did you realize they charge for room service! If I had known, I would have got up and walked over to the minibar myself. And there's Banny and the baby still trapped in China. Oh, I don't know what to do."

"I think I might just have the answer for both of us. Meet me on the corner of Ninth Avenue and Eighteenth Street in an hour. In Chelsea."

12. billy the kid

The address India gave me was an unremarkable postwar apartment building on Eighth Avenue. I wondered what this had to do with solving our financial difficulties. Perhaps she was taking me to an escort agency. I didn't know if I was comfortable with that. Oh, it's fine for *other* people. Heidi Fleiss is one of my favorite dinner guests—it's so amusing to play Guess Who's Come to Dinner with Heidi and her former clients, Charlie Sheen almost had a heart attack—but I've already mentioned my personal indifference to matters of physical intimacy.

I buzzed "Laurence, Apt. 3" as India instructed, and discreetly peeked through the iron grating of the double-locked doors to see if I could spot any of these mistresses of the night. India appeared in the hallway of the first floor. She stood in the doorway of an apartment and beckoned me to hurry. "Quickly! Quickly!" she mouthed. I pushed my way through the first door, then the second, almost tripping over the faded welcome mat. "What's all this?" I asked.

She ushered me inside a first-floor apartment, and I walked in to find a small, dark room illuminated by the glow of a computer screen. A young, slightly disheveled man sat in front of an oversize computer monitor. I presumed he was the resident "madam." Oh, well, I thought, maybe I could work the phones instead of actually "working the phones."

He didn't ask me to disrobe, however, nor did he begin to explain the finer points of running a high-class-hooker establishment. Instead the young man said, "Hi, I'm Billy Laurence."

"Excuse me?" I gasped. "Not *the* Billy Laurence?"

"The one and only," he said.

"But you're the editor of *Arbiteur!*"

"Wow, you've heard of us? I mean, of course you have," he quickly added.

Of course I'd heard about *Arbiteur.* It was an obscure online publication to the greater public at large, but one that had garnered a sure foothold among the fashion addicts of New York, Paris, and Milan, including *moi,* due to the way it incorporated streaming video, the latest technology, and the most cutting-edge editorial shoots in its sassy fashion reporting. I had stumbled across it by accident during my numerous Web searches for Stephan's website. Billy Laurence carried the longest title I'd ever encountered: CEO/editor/art director/tech support. I was shocked to find he was a wistful-looking postadolescent who didn't shave regularly and took to wearing pajamas at four o'clock in the afternoon. Not that this was rare during these babes-in-cyberland times.

"So you're Cat," Billy said happily. "India's told me so much about you." He gave me a hug and two double-cheek air kisses. "Welcome to *Arbiteur.*"

"This is it?" I cried, looking around. Billy's "office" was a cluttered desk with random computer equipment—Web cams, scanners, CPU's, laser printers. Across from his desk was a faded black leather couch where hundreds of models' look books, party invitations, and an array of press release packets touting experimental beauty regimes were piled in a haphazard manner. The fax machine was chugging away, and the television was tuned to a mute Judge Judy, while technomusic boomed in the background.

"Yes, I've found there's really no need for a very large staff to run a global fashion website."

"But this is it? Just you? What about all the names on the mast-head?"

"Imaginary," Billy admitted cheerfully. "It's something of a secret, actually, so please don't tell anybody. Otherwise the firm's credibility will be shot. After all, *Arbiteur* had its best quarter yet, and I've just landed another round of blue-chip advertising."

"Wow."

"Thank you," Billy said shyly.

India explained that several years back, Billy was a drag queen in the East Village—they first met in the bathroom of a club where Billy was in charge of giving out drink tickets to favored friends and club regulars. Billy, then known as "Miss Demeanor," was a West Coast transplant and an aspiring fashion stylist. He wrote occasional pieces for Scandinavian style magazines and helped nonprofit arts organizations stage fashion shows.

By a sheer stroke of luck, India read a small mention about *Arbiteur* in a copy of *The Wall Street Journal* that her formerly generous patron had left in her apartment. Recognizing Miss Demeanor's real name, India realized that the founder of this hot new Internet company was none other than the young drag queen who used to borrow her mascara. While I was getting my fat evaluated by a Condé Nast gatekeeper, India had looked him up and persuaded him into hiring both of us to work for his newly formed company.

"I decided I can't do everything on my own. So when India volunteered to be my eyes and ears around town, I thought, perfect," Billy explained.

"I'm going to write a gossip column called '*Depeche Merde.*' Isn't that fabulous?" India cooed.

I looked at her in awe.

"India's sure to get the scoop on the latest lesbian-model love affairs and socialite suicides," Billy said proudly. "As I remember, nobody likes dirt as much as India."

"But of course," India agreed. "I'm going to be the new media virus."

"And what am I going to do?" I asked excitedly.

India and Billy looked at each other questioningly.

"Well, that's up to you," Billy said. "What *can* you do?"

"I . . . well . . . I know how to shop," I ventured.

"You can be our market editor!" India declared. "Billy, Cat knows everything about fashion. Where to find it. How to wear it. What's in, what's out. What it's all about."

"Great. I really need someone to write show reviews during Fashion Week."

"Sure, I can do that." I nodded, although as far as writing was concerned, my experience went only as far as signing credit slips, but I was sure I could try.

"By the way, I've always been curious about the name . . . *Arbiteur*," I said. "Is it French? I thought the French for *arbiter* was *arbitre*?"

"It is?"

"Yes." I nodded.

"Oh, well, I thought *arbiter* was too harsh, so I Frenchified it. It's made-up."

"Fabulous."

"Fabulous."

We smiled at each other.

"Then it's settled," Billy said happily. "I'll expect to see you both on Monday."

"Uh, how early do I have to be here?" I asked.

"Oh, not early at all—I don't get up until about noon."

"Where are our new offices?"

"You're standing in it," he replied.

India and I looked stricken. "Isn't this apartment rather— cramped—for what we'll need to do?"

Billy shrugged. "I suppose, but I think it will serve for now." A well-worn copy of *The Millionaire Next Door* lay next to his computer.

I was chastened, but my curiosity was piqued. "But how did you start this?" I asked. "How did you get—um—funding?"

"Are you asking if I have a trust fund?" Billy laughed.

"Well—um—yes."

"No, no, no. Not at all."

"Several months ago, Billy won a settlement from his landlord," India said proudly.

"Really!"

"Yes, really," Billy said happily. "The ceiling in my bedroom collapsed due to water damage—it destroyed my stereo, my television, and just missed killing me. So I sued the bastards and won."

"And with the money, he built his own online company," India added.

"Fabulous!" I said. "Did you hire the Dream Team for your case?"

Billy shook his head.

"Cravath, Swaine and Moore? Skadden, Arps, Slater, Meagher and Flom? Dewey Ballantine?" I asked, ticking off the names of the most prestigious law firms in New York.

"More like Jacoby and Meyers," he answered humbly. "Now," he said, getting down to business. "As far as your salary is concerned, how do you girls feel about stock options?"

Under Billy's plan, India and I would waive our salaries in return for equity in the company and a generous package of stock options. Billy explained that he was planning to take *Arbiteur* public in several months, and when that happened, India, Billy and I would be newly minted dot-com gazillionaires. Until then, I could live on a line of credit secured from *Arbiteur*'s bankers.

"So I don't have any cash?" I asked Billy.

"No. No cash. Not yet," Billy replied.

"But I have equity."

"Yes, which means you'll own a part of *Arbiteur* outright."

"And stock options," I said slowly. That sounded fair enough, except I wasn't sure if illegal Chinese baby brokers accepted stock options for payment. I didn't think so.

"Yes. Those are options to buy more shares in the company at a bargain-basement price," Billy said.

"So what are those worth?" I asked skeptically.

"Well, for now, nothing," Billy explained. "They're only worth something if we get bought out or if we go public. We're going public, so they'll be worth millions. That is, if the market is good. But it will be. Most tech stocks launch with very high multiple and we could presumably have a valuation equal to LVMH."

"What's a multiple?" I asked. I had always been bad at my times tables.

"It's a . . . oh, it's too hard to explain, but just trust me . . . we're going to be huge."

"But what about the stock market?" India asked.

"What about it?"

"Isn't it a bad time for tech stocks?"

"There's nowhere it can go but up," Billy replied.

That was true enough, I thought.

"But what am I going to do for money until then?" I asked. The financial rigmarole was all too confusing.

"Simple, live on credit," Billy explained. "That's what I'm doing. We have a line of credit from our investment bank."

That I understood. Living on credit was practically my middle name. "Do you think this is a good idea?" I asked India.

"Of course, darling. It's just like therapy. You have to hit bottom to find your way out. Darkness before the light. In our case, we're going have to get *into* debt to get *out* of debt. You'll see."

Billy and India watched me closely as I wrestled with my decision, which took all of two seconds.

"Has anyone got a pen?" I finally asked.

"Here you go," Billy said happily, handing me a chewed-up Bic.

I looked at the two of them skeptically, and took in the sight of *Arbiteur*'s world headquarters: a 180-square-foot space that was so small India really had to suck it in so all of us could fit. I signed with a flourish.

"We're going to be rich!" India cheered, popping a champagne cork.

13. stealth wealth

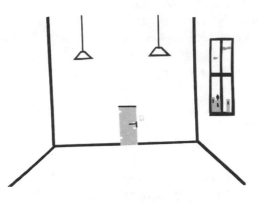

For a while there, I was fearful that by the time I finally got the money together, my baby would be old enough to audition for MTV's You Want to Be a VJ contest. Thank the Lord for *Arbiteur.* After signing the contract, I was able to withdraw a sizable personal advance on the *Arbiteur* credit line and was finally able to wire Bannerjee the amount needed to adopt my much-anticipated baby daughter. I also express-mailed Banny her brand-new visa, which the immigration lawyer I'd consulted in a run-down section of Fulton Street (his office carried the sign: "Passports/Driver's License/Green Cards/Abogado") had sold me for several thousand dollars.

"Oh, Miss Cat, the baby is so beautiful!" Bannerjee enthused during a transatlantic phone conversation after she had paid off the illegal baby brokers. "You have done a great thing, Miss Cat. The baby had nothing. All she had in the world was several dirty diapers in a brown paper bag."

I beseeched Bannerjee to bring the baby home immediately—I wanted that child out of cotton rags and in antique French lace! In preparation for my baby's arrival, I had even enrolled in a Lamaze class at Jivamukti called "Mama Yoga." So what if I wasn't actually pregnant? I still wanted to partake of all the fun things pregnancy brought. India even agreed to be my Lamaze partner. "Mama Yoga" was great—there was no jumping around, and most of the time I worked on my breathing. And God knows I already knew how to do that.

In fact, adoption had to be my best flight of fancy yet. I got to do all the fun things real moms did: yoga classes and stuffing myself with unlimited fruit smoothies without all the yucky things that came with an actual pregnancy, like elastic waistbands and flat-soled shoes.

"So when do you think you'll be home?" I asked Banny.

"Soon," Bannerjee promised. "On first flight out of here," I heard her mutter.

I considered it downright cruel to bring a child into the world and save her from a leaky orphanage and an uncertain future only to plop her down in the middle of a hotel suite, however nice the Mercer was. So, armed with a folder of documents showing I was a new partner for a hot Internet company, I bid adieu to hotel living and found a real-estate broker willing to take me around to look at apartments. Not many neighborhoods in New York are properly suitable for a down-at-the-heels self-styled fashionista/socialite.

I needed to live somewhere discreet, expensive, and charming. In the end I settled upon the cast-iron environs of the so-called "frontier neighborhood" of Tribeca and signed a lease on a new luxury loft. After all, if Mr. Bartleby-Smythe ever came to visit, he'd never dream it cost almost as much to live there as on Park Avenue. That's the wonderful thing about New York—it costs a fortune to look as if you are saving money. Mr. Bartleby-Smythe was a bit doubtful when I told him about my new *Arbiteur* credit line and our impending IPO, murmuring something that sounded like "pyramid schemes," but I didn't know what Egypt had to do with it.

Sartorially speaking, Tribeca was still the domain of the splatter-shirted and the holey-jeaned, except the new residents' intricately shredded sweatshirts were "refurbished" by popular designers whose specialty was to take frayed garments routinely found in church bin giveaways, slash them on both sides, then sew them up with brightly colored ribbon netting to produce the desired effect: "salvation irony." The kind of pseudo-low-rent wardrobe that cost six figures and goes hand in hand with condominium "lofts." Since actual dank, converted warehouse spaces were few and far between, most developers had taken to calling any three-thousand-square-foot space with fifteen-foot ceilings a loft—even though it was my under-standing that true loft-style living did not involve penthouse swim-ming pools, health clubs, and doormen. In the interests of keeping my foray into downtown living genuine, I commissioned Brother Parish, the lauded interior decorator and master of minimalism, to redesign my new apartment into a higher plane of architectural wor-thiness—to take away the embarrassingly high-end glossiness and give the space the raw, crude, art-directed edge that Melissa Stead-man's loft had displayed in *thirtysomething*.

His first order of business was to fire the painters and renovation crew I'd contracted to take care of a few minor details. I had retrieved my boxes from storage, but Brother Parish was horrified when I began to unpack. He hustled my things back into the mov-ing van and declared my apartment a "no-fly zone."

"You don't need color!" he argued with a dismissive wave of his hand.

Apparently I didn't need texture, partitions, appliances, wall hangings, furniture, blinds, photo collages, tables, chairs, rugs, and bedding either. Even the behemoth, bow-bedecked Bellini crib I had bought for the baby was relegated to the dustbin in order to create this so-called "Zen of space." Brother Parish assured me my baby would be better off, what with the dangers of SIDS and all.

"It's all just clutter!" he cried, meaning my princess bed with matching four-foot-high footstool, formaldehyde cows, and Scan-dinavian commercial oven, which he carted, peevishly, to the side-walk.

"You've been living as a bourgeois bohemian for too long," he lectured. "You don't need *things*." He grimaced. "You should have *virtual* furniture—please, join us in the twenty-first century."

Brother Parish also eliminated divisions between public and private interiors, citing obscure references to dead German philosophers. This meant both the bathroom and shower were stripped bare for all to see—making my life not unlike a November sweeps episode of *Ally McBeal*. After he was done, I had to sleep on wooden platforms in the middle of the room and watch the neighbor's television across the street with opera glasses.

"Stealth wealth," I explained to India when she came to visit the other night, and saw that my home consisted of granite, cement, exposed I beams, and raw electrical cords hanging from the ceiling.

"It's your place." India shrugged. "So where's the baby going to stay?" she asked, looking around at the wooden planks.

Oh, right. The baby. The reason I'd moved in the first place. Hmmm. "I don't know, but I'm sure I'll think of something before they get here" I said.

"Oh, well, you have anything to drink?" she asked, looking for the Sub-Zero.

I pointed to the portable coolers from Lechters that Brother Parish had approved of for their "ironic value." At least with my new *Arbiteur* credit line, I didn't have to resort to "Chandon," the California version of "Moët." I was worried what India would say if I offered her a glass of nonvintage champagne.

14. motherhood: the latest urban affectation

India and I arrived at the airport an hour before Bannerjee's plane was scheduled to arrive, so we passed the time in the airport lounge, drinking cocktails as usual. I was beginning to feel a little anxious about this new stage in my life. True, the idea had come from wanting to impress Stephan with an altruistic gesture as well as inject some meaning in my life—but now I wasn't so sure. I mean, when one goes into Barneys and purchases a knife-pleated dress but then goes home and decides one looks like an accordion, one can always *return* the offending item.

Not so a Chinese baby.

"Darling, tell me the truth, do you think I'm ready for motherhood?" I asked India nervously.

"No, of course not. Don't be silly," India scoffed.

"Well, then, maybe I can just march that tyke back to China where she belongs," I braved.

She snorted.

"I blame it all on the Chinese Orphans Society. Why throw lavish parties for the benefit of starving Chinese orphans if not to advertise their adoption?" I said, extremely agitated.

"Hmm . . ."

"Why on earth did I want to become a mother! Cody Gifford alone should have served as ample warning!" India ignored me as I continued my harangue. "Children! What was I thinking? Isn't there a money-back guarantee? After all, she's made in China. There's got to be a way!" I railed. "Everyone's infertile these days—maybe we can leave it here at the terminal? No one will know!"

I succeeded in getting her attention, but India only gave me a horrified look. "I know," I said, mortified. "I was only kidding." I tried another tactic. "Oh, but—do you think three months is too young to ship her off to Miss Porter's?" I asked innocently.

"I think it's wise if we wait until she can sit up on her own, don't you?" India stated diplomatically.

I grunted.

"Darling, you're only suffering from prepartum depression."

"What's that? And can I get a prescription for it?" I always brightened up at the thought of catching the latest affliction. All I was missing was my own personal stalker. Everyone had one these days: Dave Letterman, Madonna, Gwyneth Paltrow. What does a girl have to do to merit some harassment around here? Feel very left out as the only reasonably attractive girl in New York without a restraining order on a homicidal maniac—yet another sign that I was hopelessly in need of a comeback. Wonder if Heidi could arrange one? I must remember to ask her during our next image-rehabilitation session, I mused.

"The prenatal dumps," India explained. "You know, like the way I felt before I got Miu Miu?" Miu Miu was India's pet Maltese. "You've spent the last month waiting for this baby, it's almost here, and you're anticipating that it will be anticlimactic. You're frightened it will turn out to be incredibly disappointing."

I gripped India's arm. "Darling, I just don't know if I'm ready."

*   *   *

"Well—ready or not, here it comes," India quipped. I looked up to see an exhausted-looking Bannerjee bringing the baby toward us.

"Banny!" I hugged her tightly. "It's so good to see you again! I can't seem to find any of my Veronique Branquinho sweaters. Would you know where they are?"

Bannerjee ignored my question. "This is Boing," she said, handing me the baby.

"Boing?" I asked doubtfully. I was thinking more along the lines of "Mei-Mei," but I could live with "Boing." I was determined not to turn into one of those American mothers who ended up burdening their exotic offspring with names like Hannah or Sophie.

I steeled myself for an incredible wave of disappointment and shuddered. But when I looked down at the baby's sleeping face, I immediately fell wholeheartedly in love. A strange sensation, surely, but a nice one.

"Oh my God, she's lovely." I sighed, positively aglow with the thought of cultivating Boing's infant chic. Gucci-goo-goo booties. Power naps. Gourmet mashed bananas. ABC by APC. Alcohol-free champagne to go with Gerber's boiled carrots. I had high hopes for Boing, but I wasn't about to turn into Terry Shields. If Boing wanted to grow up to be a supermodel, an award-winning actress, or merely the premier Manhattan socialite, I wouldn't discourage her. Of course I only wanted the best for my child—several Barbara Walters interviews, maybe a liaison with a powerful man, but education was of supreme importance. I told India I wouldn't allow Boing to star in a Hollywood movie until she finished preschool.

In my mind's eye, I already had the splashy profile written and art-directed: "While the current It cradle is crowded with the likes of Presley Walker Gerber, Talita Natasha Miller von Furstenberg, and Rocco Ritchie, Boing McAllister is well on her way to similar It baby status. She causes a stir whenever her stroller is spotted at play group, and she's already adept at hiding her baby face behind a bonnet when the *babarazzi* appear. . . ."

I had to remember, however, that the burnout rate for It babies was notoriously fast. According to *Vanity Fair*, "Being an It baby is an ephemeral thing. You are only It for so long. Before you know it, another one's being born, and you're yesterday's news. The Lindbergh baby was smart—he got kidnapped. He achieved *It*-mmortality."

But my baby didn't need a ransom note—she needed a father, I thought wistfully, wondering if I would ever see Stephan again. Well, for now I would just have to be enough. After all, I had tons of parenting experience, as I had practically raised myself.

We made our way to the town car, when an airport official stopped us.

"Excuse me, ma'am, but you have not been cleared by Immigration yet. Can I see your passport?"

Bannerjee froze, then meekly handed over her passport with the brand-new visa from Fulton Street.

He looked it over carefully. "I'll need to make a copy of this. And is this your child?" he asked, meaning Boing.

"It's mine. I bough—adopted her in China," I quickly explained. "We have the receipt . . . I mean the, uh, paperwork to prove it."

"We'll have to check it out. You do know it's illegal to buy unwanted Chinese children without proper documentation," he said gravely.

Fortunately, we were ready for such a situation, and Bannerjee handed over the bogus files the shady baby brokers had given her. They testified that Bannerjee had given birth while visiting a monastery in Tibet. A false birth certificate listed one Bannerjee Bunsdaraat as the mother of Boing. How unglamorous. Instead of adopting an abandoned Chinese baby, legally I'd be known as the mother of my loyal au pair's offspring. How would I ever explain this to Boing when she grew up?

We waited with bated breath for the airport official to return with the documents.

Never knew smuggling was such an exhausting endeavor. Next

time I would just have to hire an offshore boat to row my contra-baby into the country.

"You're free to go," the customs official grunted when he returned, and handed back the papers.

We left the airport and piled into the awaiting town car. As we made our way back to Manhattan on the Cross-Bronx expressway, India noticed something odd. No, her mustache wasn't growing back.

"Why is that undistinguished Chevrolet following us?" India asked, looking out the rearview window. "They've been on our tail since we left the airport."

"What?" I asked, looking back to see a brown, standard-issue, mid-size sedan driven by a dark-suited man speaking into a wrist phone. "Hmm . . . that is strange," I agreed, but soon forgot about it as Boing had begun to cry and the three of us spent the remainder of the trip attempting to pacify her. Only India's improvisation of peekaboo (taking off and putting her wig back on her head) seemed to calm down the child.

"Home, sweet loft!" I cheered when we arrived in Tribeca.

"Miss Cat! What happened to Upper East Side?" Bannerjee cried, stricken at the sight of the rough wooden planks, the exposed ceiling, and the complete lack of furnishings.

"Don't worry, Banny, you'll adjust," India said kindly. "Look—you can heat Boing's formula with this hair dryer!"

"Is like campground!" Bannerjee complained. "No bed. No TV. No . . ."

Hmmm. Banny was right: home *was* like camp—just not the right one.

The next day, when Brother Parish arrived to check on his master-piece, he assured me roughing it would be good for the soul. I'd just never thought I'd have to rough it in my own home.

"What's this?" he asked as he cheerfully walked around the apartment looking for new things to tear apart or throw away.

He stood in front of Mummy's walk-in closet, sizing it up with a quizzical expression on his face.

"Nothing—it's nothing," I lied. "It was here when I moved in."

"Hmm . . . well, it's a waste of space and ruins the feng shui. It's got to go. Hand me the power saw."

Aieeee! I psychically restrained him from taking another step. Mummy's closet was the only thing that made my expensive camp-ground feel like home.

"Brother Parish darling, while I am perfectly content to live in a construction site, I will not abide my clothes wilting away in non-temperature-controlled air! Think of the fragile Julien Macdonald rattan sweaters! Vivien Leigh's leghorn straw hat from *Gone With the Wind!*"

"Hmmm. Oh, all right, if it means that much to you," he finally said, reluctantly putting down the chainsaw.

"Thank you, darling." Whew!

"But I'll only leave it alone if you consent to wear this while you're at home," he said. He left the room and returned holding out a shapeless beige gunnysack. "It's so you don't interfere with the look of the apartment. I had one made for Bannerjee and the baby as well."

Hmmm. Gunnysacks are awfully itchy. Being fabulous is *such* hard work.

Later that evening, Bannerjee ran into my corner, where Boing and I were peacefully sleeping on wooden floor planks, dressed in matching beige gunnysack nighties. Although Brother Parish assured me that sleeping on the floor was good for the baby, I put her in Martin Margiela's duvet coat instead. The coat was extremely soft and comfortable since it was basically a goose-down comforter.

Bannerjee shook me gently. "Miss Cat! Miss Cat!" she whispered urgently. "I think there's someone outside the door!"

"Hmmhwahmm?" I asked sleepily. "Well, let them in, then, darling."

"No—Miss Cat—come look!"

I grumpily followed Bannerjee to the peephole. A shifty-looking man dressed all in black was loitering in front of our door, speaking into his wrist phone.

Omigod. Omigod. Omigod. We were going to be killed! Robbed! Murdered in our beds . . . I mean, wooden planks.

"Should I call police?" Bannerjee asked.

"You can't!" I said, feeling doomed. "Brother Parish thinks landline phones have no place in the twenty-first century and I forgot to charge the cell phone battery."

"What we do now, Miss Cat?"

"Let me take care of it. I learned yoga self-defense at Jivamukti," I told her, getting into the Warrior One position.

"Open the door, Banny, and I'll make a downward-facing dog out of him."

"Hay-yah!" I cried.

Bannerjee opened the door with surprising force, knocking the black-clad intruder to the floor. But before we were able to restrain him, he was already up and running out of the building.

"That'll show him!" I said, even if I was still shaking. It was only when the fear had subsided that I realized . . .

"Banny—do you know what this means?"

"What Miss Cat?"

"I finally have a personal stalker! Of my very own! Isn't this fabulous?"

"Uh, OK."

"Heidi did an excellent job. I was almost terrified there—weren't you?" I asked. "It was *so* real! I thought we were finished for sure!"

I padded back into the apartment, with the cheery knowledge that my life mirrored Jodie Foster's at last.

15. fashion editrix

Never thought I would find happiness in the working world but ever since Billy Laurence hired me to be an editrix at *Arbiteur*, I'd been flush with purpose. Which was only right, since I'd had alliterative exclamations like "Lose Land's End, Go Gucci!" coursing through my veins all these years. Still, these two-hour workdays were leaving me completely drained. I'd had no idea running a global fashion magazine on the Internet would be so strenuous. I'd mistakenly assumed it was all about sauntering into tastefully appointed offices making outré pronouncements like "The End of Hip Huggers!" or "Black Is the New Black!" while an army of interns and computer programmers uploaded these statements to the server. But since there was no one on the *Arbiteur* staff but me, Billy, and India, there was more, so *much* more.

I did worry that Boing would resent my leaving her to the care of Bannerjee all day. But I knew that by working, I could teach her how to aspire to become something more than just an exquisitely turned-out beauty. She was sure to thank me when she grew up. I explained it all to her one morning.

"Now, darling," I said as I wiped drool off her face. "You know Mummy loves you but I have to work now. To make money, you know? I know, it's new to me too. But we'll have to adjust, darling. Oh, baby, don't cry, baby. I'll be home before you know it! Mummy loves you!" I sobbed as I ran out of the loft and into the waiting town car.

Note to self: ask Billy about the possibilities of telecommuting.

When I arrived Billy was wearing pajamas with little ducks on them. His hair was rumpled, and, as usual, he badly needed to shave.

"Billy darling," I said tentatively.

"Yes, Cat?" he asked with a big yawn.

"Perhaps we can let some air in here?" I asked. "It's rather stuffy."

"Oh—sure," he said, turning on the air conditioner. It wasn't quite what I was looking for but I had warmed to Billy's little eccentricities. He was an extraordinarily cheerful man, and an incredibly accommodating boss—he never batted an eye even when I waltzed into work at three in the afternoon.

I sat myself down on the leather couch across from his desk. Billy had kindly moved the leather-bound model look books and other fashion detritus to the floor to give me a "work space." When India arrived, she took her usual place on the armrest of the couch next to me, giggling to herself while viciously typing away on a laptop computer. This week, her column's blind item involved a scribe who had peed into the closet of his boss's home in a drunken stupor.

We sat quietly for a while, Billy blinking at the computer while I looked through several dozen model books to find the right girl for my first *Arbiteur* shoot. The doorbell buzzed. Exciting. I went to answer it, fully expecting a messenger bearing another model's portfolio or brown paper bags filled with the beauty products I'd ordered, or else new clothing samples for our run-through. Instead, I opened the door to find a deliveryman wearing an orange jumpsuit and a kooky hat. He was holding a copy of *Runaway Bride* and a pint of Ben & Jerry's Chunky Monkey.

"That's for me, thanks," Billy said, taking the items.

"Oh."

Billy dug into his ice cream.

"A breakfast ice cream," India noted dryly.

After Billy had his breakfast, we convened for our weekly ideas meeting, when we planned the website's features and decided which fashion moments to showcase on our web pages: the next trend, the next designer, the next idea, the next celebrity interview. The result of our decisions would affect the entire course of fashion for a day, a week, even a millennium! The stress was enormous, which is why during our meetings, Billy, India, and I always consumed several bottles of wine to help the flow.

Billy opened the meeting with the standard question: "Anybody got any ideas?"

India and I looked at each other blankly.

"Um . . ."

"Um . . ."

"I have an idea!" India said.

"You do?" Billy asked excitedly. "Share, share!"

"I've been thinking . . . I can't possibly go on as India anymore!" she cried.

"What does this have to do with our weekly features?" Billy asked in befuddlement. Obviously, nothing—but then, wasn't that what editorial ideas meetings were for? Last week at the ideas meeting, India, Billy, and I had debated the merits of snooty sales clerks at several illustrious designer boutiques and whether the fat-free Bundt cake we ordered for breakfast from the corner deli was *actually* fat-free.

India ignored him, getting up to stick a manicured fingernail in our faces. "India! India! *India!* Every fucking clerk at Barneys or waitress at Balthazar or blow-job queen from Lotus is named *fucking India!*"

"India Beresford-Givens is a lovely name!" I scolded her. "And may I point out you didn't even have to make it up? Really. You're so fortunate."

"Ladies?"

"Yes?"

"Can we get back to our ideas meeting now?" Billy asked, all business. "Now, which underage movie star are we going to feature on our splash page *this* week?"

We finally settled on a budding child actress whom no one had ever heard of but who had recently appeared in her underwear in a high-profile movie for ten minutes. This was a brilliant inspiration on my part—equal to putting Gretchen Mol and Heath Ledger on the cover of, oh, just about any magazine. I was nothing if not a firm advocate for the creation of more dubious, quasifamous celebrities—especially since I was one—more Lisa Marie Presleys, more Debi Mazars, more Carson Dalys. More, more, more! I knew the world couldn't get enough of pretty people who went to parties. What else could explain numerous magazine pictorials documenting the shopping habits of Jennifer Tilly?

"Now, darlings, I'd love to stay, but I've got to make my rounds of celebrity garbage. Ta." India's *"Depeche Merde"* column routinely featured the latest from stars' dust bins, through a sidebar called "Rubbish of the Rich and Famous," wherein empty yogurt containers, DVD cardboard boxes, and used prophylactics were analyzed and critiqued by a panel of psychiatrists and assorted experts.

"Hey, Billy, I've got an idea. You'll love it," I told him once India had left.

"OK, shoot."

"You know how we run all these pictures of Ginny Bond, Lauren du Pont, and Serena Altschul in Party Patrol?"

"Yes?"

"I was thinking—we don't really need to see all their faces again, do we? I mean, they're already covered to death in every other magazine. Why not do something different?"

"OK, what do you have in mind?"

With Billy's reluctant blessing, from that day forward, the only self-promoting fashionista/socialite featured in our society pages would be yours truly. Me at the opening of the ballet, me at the movie premiere, and me *again* shopping for endive in London's hip Portobello market! Saving *Arbiteur* thousands in paparazzi costs, and bolstering my own status in the celebrity-socialite nexus! It would be just like the short-lived but seminal publication *Ivana: Living in Style*, except with me, not Ivana. That would show Teeny she wasn't the only one who could smile prettily into a camera while affecting an air of supreme insouciance.

"Now," I said to Billy. "Where do you keep the fashion closet around here?"

"Oh, it's over there, through the kitchen and next to the bathroom. Why?" he asked.

"I just thought I could work better, if it was in my apartment. You don't mind, do you, Billy?" I followed his directions and was impressed to find the dining room had been converted into a well-stocked fashion closet—I spied Balenciaga ball gowns, Bruce denim jackets, even Tuleh feather boas. Perfect! I immediately called to confirm my appointment with the movers. Before Billy could protest, my boys were inside the apartment, lifting racks of coats, sweaters, goat-fur Gucci, and shelves of Christian Louboutin, Alain Tondowski, and Sigerson Morrison heels.

"Let's go, boys—lift those racks! Careful of the white Helmut Lang pantsuits!"

Billy looked confused at first, then he shrugged. "Oh, well, I guess it's better if I have a place to eat, anyway."

After I sent the movers to Tribeca, and the fashion closet was relocated in my own, I made the rounds of designer showrooms. Little-known but cutting-edge fashion outlets like ours routinely served as incubators for up-and-coming designers who had yet to see a stitch of theirs in the pages of *Vogue*. Visiting a showroom was the most crucial part of a market editor's job, when she takes her team (in this case, there was only one member: *moi*) to see the new collections up close and talk to designers about their fresh ideas. Ideas are *mucho importante* in fashion. Why, without ideas we wouldn't have ideas meetings. Fashion designers are an incredibly sweet bunch, I found. I simply walked into their showrooms and they handed me a steamer trunk filled with the entire collection.

"Ooh, this isn't in my size," I pouted to a scruffy-headed neophyte designer who was dying to get his papier-mâché jackets and burnt jeans into *Arbiteur*'s next shoot.

"It's not? Terrence!" he barked at his assistant. "Make sure next time you give Cat the fours." To me, he said, "I'm so sorry about that. It won't happen next time."

"It's fine," I said graciously. "Don't think two seconds about it."

"So the clothes will be in the next shoot?" he asked.

"I'll have to talk to Billy about it—but I don't see why not." I smiled.

He gave me a great big hug and an extra steamer trunk full of clothes. Next time I'd have to bring a flatbed truck with me as there was simply not enough space in the town car for all the loot.

I mean, *ideas*.

The day's bounty secured in my loft, I brought back a few random pieces that weren't quite my style to show to Billy. Unfortunately, since I had kept almost all the clothes, there wasn't much left for the model to wear.

"So you're sure there wasn't anything in the showroom that was worthy other than these frilly pantaloons?" he asked.

"Nothing." I shook my head innocently. "Well, that's all I have for today," I told him, looking at my watch. It was almost time to meet India for our usual late-afternoon lunch at the hip new boîte in SoHo. I followed the rigorous schedule of fashion editors everywhere—a short morning meeting, a bountiful trip to a designer's showroom, followed by a three-hour lunch at the most exclusive restaurant in town.

"All righty, then. I'll see you tomorrow?"

"You're not coming to lunch?" I asked, surprised. "It's the hot new place. I don't know about the food, but everyone will be there."

"Oh, I'm not much for eating out," Billy explained. "I usually just order a turkey sandwich from the deli."

"All right," I said. It suddenly occurred to me that I'd never seen Billy outside the confines of his home/office. I wondered if he ever went outside. He was rather pale, in an appealing Joaquin Phoenix way, without the cleft lip.

The restaurant was a popular haven for pushy types from both old and new media. One prominent magazine editor who was told it would be a forty-five-minute wait stomped off in a huff. I had no such problem, however, as India had slept with the maître d' and was already waiting for me at a corner table when I arrived.

I looked around the restaurant to see who else was there, and noticed Teeny across the way. She caught my eye and gave me the usual crooked wave with her fashion finger, which I reluctantly returned. Teeny stood up and her lunch date, whose back was turned to us, got up as well and helped her dutifully with her coat. As they walked toward the door, I caught a glimpse of her broad-shouldered companion. He had blond hair and was wearing a beautiful, slim-cut three-button suit. Then I saw the eye patch.

It was Stephan! My heart sank and I immediately hid myself behind a menu. India kicked me under the table as they walked past us on their way out of the restaurant.

"He's not with her," India hissed. "It's just *lunch*. Lunch is nothing. Lunch is . . . lunch is . . . not romantic. Lunch is casual. Lunch is not a *date*. If he were really into her, he would be taking her to *dinner*. Now, dinner. That's a *sign*."

"India, I love you to death, but don't you see? It's hopeless. I'm not good at this kind of thing. If he wants to be with her, fine. I really don't care anymore. Liking someone is too icky. Too much trouble," I blustered. "It gives me minuscule frown lines and makes me want to throw up—and you know I'm not supposed to do that anymore." Inside, I was dying—*dying*. Had he taken her to see his upside-down view of the city as well? Were they together? They *had* to be. Teeny wasn't one to waste her time with men who couldn't help her with the bottom line.

I should have stood up and said hello, at least, but like I said, I wasn't built for uncomfortable situations. Instead, I swallowed my disappointment and hid behind a menu. Besides, I told myself bravely, there were more important things to worry about. It was that time again on the Fashion Calendar—New York Fashion Week!

16. live from bryant park

Aaah, New York Fashion Week. That magical time twice a year when hundreds of journalists, buyers, boutique owners, and celebrities from around the world converge upon a small, citywide block to watch the latest collections. Five glorious days of champagne, air kisses, and goodie bags! And this time I was part of the circus! In charge of reporting on the latest in the world of style. Jeanne Becker—watch your back! Suzy Menkes—eat my dust! Fashion wasn't just a lifestyle choice anymore, it was also going to pay the bills; and what big bills they were. *Arbiteur*'s investment bankers told us that our IPO was scheduled for next month—and not a moment too soon. I was seriously overextended on the *Arbiteur* credit line.

"Where the hell are you?" an agitated India asked, calling my cell the morning of the first day of Fashion Week.

"I'll be there in seconds," I answered, as I didn't want her to think I was slacking off on the job.

"The show has started without you. And Billy wants to know if you remembered to bring the digital video camera."

Oops.

"I'll go back and get it."

"No—forget it, we'll just steal the streaming video off the Cat-walk.com website. They'll never know."

"OK."

"Where are you?"

I looked out the window and to my horror I saw the Statue of Liberty in the distance instead of the Empire State Building.

"We're at the tents, miss," the chauffeur announced.

"India, I'm at Battery Park!" Apparently the fool driver had mistaken the Big Apple Circus tents downtown for the 7th on Sixth tents in Midtown's Bryant Park, which twice a year becomes the absolute center of the fashion universe.

I gave the driver a talking-to and he was about to turn the car around when I spotted a designer outlet store around the corner. "Hold on!" I told him. Hmmm. Might as well pop in while I was down here. After all, the more I bought, the more I saved! I promised India I'd be at the show as soon as possible, but not until I checked out the outlet store's offerings. After all, wasn't fashion coverage all about shopping? Our readers would no doubt benefit from this excursion!

Egads. Three o'clock already. Half of the day's shows were already over, and I hadn't even set foot in the correct tents yet. But the day was not wholly wasted: I was now the proud owner of several exquisite pieces purchased at a glorious discount. When I finally arrived at Bryant Park, I hid my bags from India, who was waiting for me on the entrance steps to the main tent. The tent doors were guarded vigilantly by a real "fashion police" force, a private security firm that checked invitations and press credentials before allowing one into the hallowed ground.

India was trying very hard to have Bill Cunningham from *The New York Times* take her picture. Bill stood ten feet away from where India was affecting an apathetic manner, although she was outrageously outfitted in an attention-grabbing, multicolored sheared mink coat, bright leather chaps, and a gargantuan cowboy hat. Unfortunately, Bill was just as oblivious to India as she pretended to be to him.

When India finally gave up on capturing his attention, she nodded to the guard, who allowed her inside, and I attempted to follow her but the guard physically blocked my entrance with his body.

"Identification, please!" he roared.

"I'm here for the shows—I'm with *Arbiteur*!" I argued.

"Where's your invitation?"

I searched inside my overstuffed handbag for my invitation. MP3 player, wallet, cell phone, beeper, Palm Pilot, tape recorder, receipts from the day's shopping excursion. But no lacy G-string with my seat assignment on it. ("Welcome," it read on the crotch.) Terribly disturbing, as I had expressly given Bannerjee direct orders to prepare my handbag for Fashion Week, and I was sure I had told her not to forget the invitations.

"What about an ID or a press pass?" the door goon grunted.

But I never carried an ID for fear of revealing my real age! And neither Billy nor India had mentioned I needed a press pass. India gave me a frustrated look from the other side and I gestured for her to go on ahead.

"Here—what about this?" I asked, showing him an "international student ID" acquired in college for pre-twenty-one drinking binges.

No dice.

"Can I at least sit at the café?" I asked, meaning the outdoor reception area where the Moët & Chandon flowed freely. This was a perk provided by the organizers to help the fashion folk recover from "a hard day of shows." I was already exhausted but had yet to see one anorexic model in an unwearable creation slouch down the runway to neo-Gregorian ambient jungle trip-hop.

"All right," he growled.

Who needs to see a fashion show when one can drink champagne? I eyed the canapés on the tray and glanced around to see if anyone was looking in my direction.

"Hey there, you," a familiar voice called.

I looked up, in mid-cucumber-sandwich crunch. "Stephan!" I exclaimed. "What are you doing here?" The fashion shows had become very popular among well-heeled businessmen of all types, who usually finagled tickets through corporate sponsors. They regarded the shows as the newest spectator sport. This suit-and-cell-phone crowd could be spotted at any high-profile media event: ringside at heavyweight boxing matches at Atlantic City, courtside at Madison Square Garden during the play-offs. During Fashion Week they could usually be counted on to ogle models from the front rows, seated in between the rows of disdainful editors and distressed buyers from department stores, who had the thankless job of selling the public on three-armed sweaters and diaphanous daywear.

"A friend of mine invited me to a show, and I thought I'd pop in during my lunch hour," he explained. "Why aren't you inside? I came too late and they had given my seat away."

"I was running late as well. I'm here for *Arbiteur,*" I explained.

"What's *Arbiteur?*"

"It's a new fashion website. We're *quite* influential; I'm surprised you haven't heard of us," I chided.

"Forgive me?" he teased.

"Anyway, I just needed something to do," I said airily. "It's not like a job or anything. . . ."

"Oh, of course." He nodded. "And how's the baby?"

"Boing."

"Excuse me?"

"Her name is Boing," I said defensively. "It's an ancient Chinese name."

"Interesting choice." He grinned. "It's very distinctive."

"And for your information, she's fine, thanks."

"So," he paused, looking at me with those piercing eyes. "Where did you disappear to? I went to visit you but your doorman said you had moved to the Mercer Hotel. But when I called there they said you had checked out. So I called Information, but you're not listed."

"I know, I'm so sorry. I've moved to a loft in Tribeca. Have you heard of Brother Parish? The interior decorator? He's rearticularized my space into a dichotomy of form and function," I babbled, trying to remember what Brother Parish had said. "Brother Parish hates clutter. He's very minimalist. I can't put anything anywhere, because he designed all the surfaces in the apartment to have a slight tilt—if I stack magazines and papers on them, they fall to the floor. That's minimalism for you."

He laughed, and his one good eye crinkled charmingly. "You're insane."

"I'm intriguing," I retorted.

He smiled and I sipped my champagne. He hovered nearer. Our champagne glasses clinked, and I slowly closed my eyes. This time I would get it right. It's amazing—the last time I was this infatuated it was with a pair of knee-high snakeskin boots, and I *knew* they would be mine. I could smell the sweetness of his breath, a mixture of cigarettes and champagne and Aqua di Parma. Then . . .

"Excuse me!"

Stephan and I turned in annoyance. It was a photographer holding up a large camera. "Can I take your picture?" he asked, pointing to me. Once the other lensmen noticed their colleague taking my picture, they all began snapping photographs as well, and soon I was blinded by a torrent of flashbulbs.

"Oh, of course," I complied, elated. It was about time! The incessant coverage of myself in *Arbiteur*'s "Party Patrol" must have finally elicited interest from the mainstream press. Of course, it could also have been due to their haste to capture my outfit—I was wearing Viktor & Rolf's Fall/Spring 2000—the *entire* collection all at once (which was how they suggested it be worn), which made me look not unlike a Russian doll. The phalanx of photographers pushed Stephan away and soon he was lost in the stream of the stiletto-heeled who had flooded into the champagne bar once the show had ended. I strained to find him and was about to call out when I noticed he was making his way toward Teeny, whom I noticed standing behind the tent doors. I guessed she was the "friend" who had invited him to the show.

"What happened to you?" India asked when she found me slumped against the bar.

"I got a little sidetracked," I said offhandedly. I promised myself I would file my first review for *Arbiteur* tomorrow. Right, tomorrow.

Urrrgggh. Why was the baby screaming? At six in the morning? *Must* impress upon child not to wake up to be fed, I thought. It's too common to want to eat. What will people say? Really, it's too distracting, especially as I'm a working mother now.

I padded over to the crib and gave her a bottle. "There you go; happy now?" I asked.

Boing chortled and cooed, slurping hard.

Oh well. What could you do? I gave her a kiss. *Kids.*

In truth, I was obsessed with the baby. I couldn't buy enough little sailor outfits from Jean Paul Gaultier Enfants. And India, well, you'd never think New York's first aristocratic transsexual would feel maternal, but not only had India agreed to be a godmother, she was already planning the christening. There would be clowns, fireworks, and the Reverend Al Sharpton officiating. But I wasn't even sure I was Christian. My father was a lapsed Catholic and my mother worshiped at the altar of Kenneth. The way I saw it, choosing a religion was like wearing underwear: you should try on a different one every day. I'd done the Hindu thing, the Buddhist thing, the Shanti-Astangi. I'd found enlightenment and I didn't even *wear* underwear—I was fabric-sensitive as a child.

I was so glad I was now employed, as I really had to start saving my pennies for the baby. I could send a whole Sri Lankan village to medical school for the price of kindergarten at Dalton!

"Well, you know," India had suggested. "There's always . . ."

But there was no way. Even if it meant debtor's prison. I just couldn't. I'd heard they let *anyone* enroll. Scandalous! In my mind, education should involve such things as Peter Pan collars, vespers, and French carols sung in the belvedere, *not* metal detectors, transparent backpacks, and automatic-weapon-wielding preteens. India retorted that even if I sent Boing to private school, she'd still have to pass some test.

"Test? What test?" I had asked.

"Admissions tests, silly. You don't think they let just anyone into Dalton, do you? And anyway, Miss Hoity-Toity, Stuyvesant is even harder to get into than Dalton and it's a public school."

But I wasn't worried about Boing; she was Chinese. Everyone knows they're smart.

This time I was out of the house in time for John Bartlett's eleven o'clock presentation. I was disturbed to find out that as an editor at *Arbiteur*, I was assigned a standing-room seat! Standing-room tickets were traditionally ferreted out to fashion students and distant relatives of the designer. But no matter, it wasn't like I didn't know how to upgrade to the knocking-on-heaven's-door environs of a dignified "section A, row 1, seat 10" with some help from whiteout and a pen.

I breezed through the lines, waving my forged ticket above my head, and found an empty front-row seat. Turning to the program's "run of show" I skimmed the names of the models walking on the runway and counted two Ashleys, three Tiffanys, four Marie-Annes, and one of each of the following: Lavinia, Luvigna, Lagina, Listagna, Laeticia, Ljupka, Ludmilla, Yfke, Rifke, Neitschze, Serenna, Corinna, Fromilla, Tange, Unge, Fungi, Gisele, Mimi, Maggie, Krissie, Irina, Komiko, Tynk, Wink, Stink, Cordova, Maldova, Magnolia, Maglosia, Alek, and Carolyn.

The lights went down, the booming music started, and the show was beyond marvelous—more nipples than *Showgirls*. Everything falling off the shoulder or plunging deep into crevices. I trembled with excitement and wrote down notes, which I saw other fashion editors doing. Next to me solemn-faced women scribbled furiously in their notebooks, while others spoke softly into Dictaphones. "Yellow." "Orange." "Ruffles." "Disco." "Feathers." "Strapless." "Nude." "Guerrilla." "Urban."

This is what I wrote in mine: "Apocalyptic." "Unreal." "Hazardous." "Must remember to take in dry cleaning."

When the last guerrilla-glamazon walked down the runway, John Bartlett came out to take his bows, as usual, holding his pet dog Sweetie in his arms. Sweetie was something of a trendsetter herself, as the glamour pooch columnist of *Elle* magazine. This was something of a sore point for India, since her Maltese Miu Miu was just as cute but had yet to make *one* stylish pronouncement. The back row, filled with the front-row editors' assistants, FIT (Fashion Institute of Technology) students, and assorted gate crashers, gave him a standing ovation, while everyone else clapped politely. No one ever dared show any enthusiasm for a collection no matter how fabulous. A look of boredom, disdain, and downright loathing was almost mandatory. Unless, of course, you were a certain white-haired emeritus fashion director who was famous for her audible gasping, rolling about in the aisles, and literal jumping for joy if she liked something on the runway.

India and I collected our seat candy—travel-size containers of body lotion, and the expensive, useless tchotchke given as a token of esteem from the designer to the fashion press. Any interest in the goodie bags is *très* gauche—although even unflappable front-row denizens have been known to squeal in delight when a particularly choice freebie was found on their seat (Louis Vuitton and Prada were famous for gifting front-row editors with actual bags worth several thousand dollars during show presentations).

"Hair spray and condoms!" India whispered, peeking inside the bag. "Hooray!"

"I'm going backstage to troll for some goss," India said. "Come with?"

"No, I've got to file my report." I demurred, as I was secretly hoping I'd run into Stephan at the champagne bar again. I waited for a few minutes, but when I didn't see him anywhere, I repaired to the journalists' lounge next to the café and was thrilled to discover it had all the makings of an uptown day spa. There were paraffin hand treatments for those whose fingers were exhausted from all that writing, facials for those who had frowned too much, and foot massages to combat the stress of walking from taxi to tent. I nixed the beauty treatments as I had *real* work to do, and uploaded my three-word rave of John Bartlett's show on the *Arbiteur* website, next to the stolen streaming video from Catwalk.com. Not a minute later, my cell phone rang.

"*Arbiteur,*" I answered crisply. "This is Cat."

"Your show review—one word: *gorge,*" Billy crowed.

This was easier than I thought! Wondered what Teeny would say when she saw my byline on *Arbiteur.* I was also planning a critical investigation into Tart Tarteen's business practices as my first fashion exposé.

"And I have great news—we've won the award for best fashion website from the Nettie Awards!"

"What's that?" I asked.

"It's like the Oscars of the Internet."

"They have those?"

"Yes. Apparently they can't get enough of India's gossip column, and you know that fashion shoot you styled? The one called 'Castoffs' with the antique bloomers? They said it was genius!"

"So what did we win?"

"A coiled statuette that looks like a Slinky. Cat, this is a milestone for *Arbiteur.* A huge achievement. We're going to get extreme recognition and it's great news for our IPO."

The next day I was determined to wake up early to arrive on time for Miguel Adrover's show, which I promised Billy I would not miss. Like other "rebellious" downtown designers, Miguel wasn't showing at the tents but at a morgue downtown. I was badly hungover from the aftershow parties of the night before. Oh well, fashion shows were notorious for their late starts. The audience at Marc

Jacobs's show two days earlier was probably still waiting for the lights to dim.

I kissed Boing good-bye, and feeling very much like a hard-charging editrix of an award-winning global fashion website, I climbed into the car with a renewed sense of purpose.

"Grand and Jackson, please, driver."

En route, I pondered a question that had been nagging me for days. Was I turning into a champagneaholic? The same fatal disease that afflicted waif supermodels and grunge rock goddesses? I looked up the symptoms for Bubbly Overdose Syndrome from the latest copy of *Dr. Feelnothing's Guide to Designer Diseases*.

Let's see . . . "Pavlovic reaction to popping corks." Yes!

"Inability to distinguish Joe Pesci from Kosovar busboys at night-clubs." Was that Joe Pesci India and I were partying with last night, or a recent Kosovar immigrant? *I don't know, I don't know!*

"Middle fingers in carpal-tunnel cramp from holding flute glass." I attempted to wiggle my fingers but couldn't feel them! I was suffering from the syndrome for certain!

But then the phone rang and I was able to answer it without any effort or pain. Hmmm.

"Hello, Cat darling."

"Hello, India sweetheart."

"All ready for Miguel's show?"

"Oh, most definitely. I look smashing. I'm wearing my Louis Vuitton garment bag," I told her, explaining I had slashed and stitched my logo luggage into a suitable one-piece in homage to the designer, who had done the same thing in his first, groundbreaking collection. As India chatted away, I looked idly out the window. Wait a minute! I knew Manhattan's Lower East Side wasn't the prettiest part of town, but this didn't even look like Manhattan at all! Where were the newly chic Orchard Street bars and parvenu dress shops next to Jewish delicatessens and turn-of-the-century sweatshops?

"Is this Grand and Jackson?" I asked the driver.

"Yes, ma'am. This is Queens." Apparently the fool driver had mistaken the directions for an intersection in the most unglamorous of boroughs.

Nooooooo! "India—I'm in Queens! I know—it's *rich*. I'll send postcards, but, darling, I can't talk now!" I folded the phone and started to hyperventilate. Billy had expressly instructed me to deliver show coverage for Miguel Adrover's line. The driver professed to know a quick shortcut back to Manhattan, and even though I had my reservations, I let him use it.

Hours later I rang India. From *Brooklyn*. Quick shortcut turned into major gridlock detour and I was just as far from Manhattan and Fashion Week as ever.

"So, how was Miguel's?"

"Fantastic. You know how last season he did '*Midtown*'?"

"Yes?"

"Well, this season, he did '*Outer Borough*.' It was disturbing and divine. Oh, Cat, you're so lucky to be in Brooklyn. So fashion-forward of you."

For the last day of Fashion Week, everybody's favorite rap-mogul-turned-menswear-designer threw a birthday party for himself—one that was even more expensive than mine! Of course, I was not invited, but that's never stopped me before. I desperately wanted to go because I thought for sure Stephan would be there, since he never seemed to miss a fabulous event. For the party, each of the two thousand guests had been given a VCR tape that played key scenes from the rap star's life, complete with a soundtrack. The location was kept secret until the very last minute, and India had to torture a caterer to find out the secret password. When we arrived, the crowd was so thick that the publicists were turning even bona-fide celebrities away.

A proper invitation and a *Vogue* cover don't guarantee anything when it comes down to it. If an event proves too popular, publicists have been known to actually disinvite guests who have already RSVP'd. But even if you clear the preparty politics, there is still the matter of actually getting inside the event. If the venue is grossly overcrowded and already in violation of fire laws, and the crowd outside the door is filled with the likes of the Duchess of York, the Princess of Greece, and the King of Pop—well, those with less-than-stellar credentials—and I don't care how many *Tiger Beat* covers you've been on—not that I've ever been a *Tiger Beat* cover girl—you don't get inside.

I spotted Brick and his arm-candy date arguing loudly after being turned away at the door. Pasha was berating him for their debilitating social humiliation.

"Cunnnot you do something?" she screeched. "Owlof my friends are olllready inside. It's *theee* pahty of the week. I cunnnot mees eeet."

"Sorry, babe. I tried my best," Brick apologized. "I don't understand; Enrico promised me he'd get us on the list," he added, annoyed and flustered. Brick wasn't used to having people say no to him; it just wasn't done.

"Ugh! This is soooo not cool, Breeck." She pouted, then stalked off in a funk.

"Hi, darling." I waved. "Having a bit of trouble there?"

"Oh, hi, Cat," he said sheepishly. "It's nothing—she'll get over it." He ran after her, calling out her name in the dark. "Pasha? Pasha doll? Come on! I've got a contact who can get us into the Chaos party! Don't leave me!" He ran off after her, their footsteps fading into the night.

The sidewalk was filled with other supermodel casualties—Lavigna, Ljupka, Ashley, Irina, Trish, and Teena-Marie had not been allowed in either. They wandered around aimlessly, like lost little children without a party to attend, cell phones glued to their ears, complaining noisily in a hodgepodge of accents.

"Incroyable!"

"Vere ees next partee?"

"Casablancas-san, me no get in."

There was a lovely little bar right next to the event, but no one even thought of abandoning ship and going there. It was the principle of the thing. To actually pay for a night out was outside the typical model's earthly existence. They were very fragile, and withered at the sight of a drink bill.

Fortunately for us, the girl at the door was one of the few fashion addicts who had actually heard of *Arbiteur.* "You're Cat McAllister!" she squealed when she noticed me in the crowd.

"I've seen you in that 'Party Patrol' column," she explained.

"You have?"

"Oh, it's my favorite website. And is this . . . ?" she asked, motioning to India.

"India Beresford-Givens—she writes '*Depeche Merde,*'" I said proudly.

"You guys are the best! I'm such a big fan! *Arbiteur* is like the best-kept secret in the fashion industry."

We smiled benevolently. "Can we get through now?"

"Totally!" she said, raising the velvet rope. "Hey—who's the blind item in your gossip column last month? The drunken journalist who peed in the closet of his boss's home? Was it Michael Musto?"

India gave her an enigmatic smile. "We'll never tell."

"India, I can't believe nobody's guessed that it was you!" I whispered.

Once inside, I immediately spilled champers down Martha Stewart's back. India gave her advice on how to clean it, from an article in Martha's magazine. It was a splendid party—all the right people, and names, names, names, but Stephan was nowhere to be found. Shame, I felt myself blush at the memory of that almost-kiss. He had been about to kiss me, hadn't he? Or did I just have something on my chin? It had been so long since I had actually kissed anybody. Brick and I—well, who cared about that anymore?

17. they'll always have paris

Um, Cat, before we have our editorial meeting today, can I talk to you about your New York Fashion Week coverage?" Billy asked in a serious tone.

"Oh? Why?" I felt a glimmer of fear. Was I being fired so soon after my debut? Not even when I read for the role of Gertie in *E.T.* had I been hustled out of a position so soon.

"Please don't take this the wrong way—your coverage of John Bartlett's show was fantastic."

"Thank you, I did try." Relief flooded over me.

"And the fact that we've asked our stringers in Paris, Milan, and London to cover the European collections doesn't bear *any* judgment at all on the job you've done," he continued. Hmm . . . I was wondering about that. I had fully expected to follow the fashion pack across the Atlantic for the rest of the fashion season, but Billy convinced me I was needed at *Arbiteur* HQ.

"Besides, I don't think we can afford to pay your expenses in Italy." Billy had been less than thrilled when I handed him the bill for the "discounted" designer items I had picked up during my Fashion Week detour.

"I'd hate to see what would happen when you discover the Prada outlet," he joked.

Did he say Prada outlet? I'd been *robbed*.

"There is, however, the question of Couture Week in Paris. Against my better judgment, I find I have no one to send but you and India to cover the shows. But only if you promise not to go on any more shopping sprees."

"I'd love that!" I breathed, knowing that Teeny was sure to be in Paris as well, since she never missed a couture show. It was the lifeblood of her Tart Tarteen line, as she was notorious for getting lower-priced versions of the fantastic, otherworldly creations from the runways into the stores immediately. And if Teeny were there—would Stephan be far behind?

"Cat, Cat? So it's all right, yes?"

"Yes."

"Great."

"What's great?" I asked blankly.

"My one tiny suggestion?" Billy asked in an exasperated tone.

"Yes? What was it again? I'm sorry, I didn't hear you very well the first time."

Billy looked a tad uncomfortable. "Well, all I meant was that since there will be several designers showing—meaning *more than one*—I just thought it might be better for our readers and, well, the purposes of our website, if, well . . . if . . ."

"If?"

"If when you go to Paris, you were able to report on more than one designer. Don't get me wrong, I adore John Bartlett—but . . . well, anyway, do you think you could do that?"

I tittered. "Of course, darling! Why, all you needed to do was ask!"

"Great." Billy smiled.

Later, as I was sorting the day's mail at the office, I stumbled upon a rather distressing letter addressed to *Arbiteur* from Catwalk.com.

"Billy darling!" I called when I saw it. "Have you seen this?" I waved the official-looking envelope.

Billy looked up from his morning coffee at three o'clock in the afternoon. "Mmmm?" He squinted at it. "Is it another cease-and-desist letter from Catwalk.com?"

"How did you know?"

"Oh, they sent us one last season. For stealing their streaming video." He yawned. "I thought we would get our own coverage this year, but . . ." I flushed, remembering how I had forgotten to bring the digital video camera with me to the recent New York fashion shows.

"What are we going to do?" I asked nervously. "It looks like they mean business. They're threatening some kind of lawsuit," I said, skimming the document. "Do you want me to call a lawyer?"

"Nah," Billy said, waving the notion away. "They'll never get around to actually suing us. Don't worry about it."

"If you're sure," I said, putting the letter away in the Out box, which doubled as Billy's CD tower. It looked ominous and oppressive, but after a couple of days, I forgot all about it.

I promised Billy when India and I left for Paris that I wouldn't try to do anything too extreme. "And remember—try to report on more than one show!" he called as the car drove us away.

Unlike the pret-a-porter collections, couture clothing—custom-made, one-of-a-kind creations that take two weeks to two months to finish—was relevant only to a handful of women around the globe. Those who could afford hundred-thousand-dollar evening dresses that take a team of ten hunchbacked women four months to make. Due to the sorry state of my finances, I hadn't been able to afford couture in a while, but thanks to *Arbiteur's* upcoming IPO, this was all going to change immediately.

For the trip, I FedExed my wardrobe ahead. It's so inconvenient to cart around baggage—emotional or otherwise. I called Boing several times from the airplane, as I missed her already. Bannerjee mentioned the mysterious stalker was still skulking around the perimeter, talking into his wrist phone, but I told her not to worry, as he was probably harmless, although I did make a note to tell Heidi to call him off, since it was all well and good for my image for me to be so regularly harassed, but it wouldn't do to have him scaring my au pair.

India and I checked into our adjoining suites in the Ritz. I asked the concierge if Mummy was registered, as I knew she never missed Couture Week, and was sorely disappointed to find she had left for Acapulco.

We were thrilled to find that Billy had thoughtfully alerted the hotel staff to our presence, as we found our rooms lavishly appointed with flowers, champagne, caviar, smoked salmon, and other tasty nibblies. India had just popped the cork when the concierge entered our room in a state of extreme agitation.

"Ah, mademoiselles," he said, wiping his palms together nervously. "Eees zome meestake, no? *Vous n'êtes pas Na-ooh-meee Campbell?*"

Since neither of us were currently being sued by our former employees for cell phone abuse, we both shook our heads.

"Aaahhh . . . I zought zo. Pliss, eees vairy importante. Eeez not your rooomz."

"Come again?"

"Your rooomz down zee hall . . . thair . . . plisss follow me."

India and I exchanged distressed looks and we started babbling numerous threats and imprecations at the funny little man.

"Why, I never!"

"We're *press*, mind you. If you ever want anyone to stay here again—"

"Our editor will hear of this!"

"Impossible. I've already unpacked. You can't expect me to—"

The concierge shook his head and bowed out the door. We heard him trying to explain the situation to someone in the hallway, but he was suddenly cut off by an agonized scream, and what sounded suspiciously like a cell phone being thrown at his head.

* * *

Unlike at 7th on Sixth, the couture collections were shown in various locations around Paris. We scurried from out-of-the-way train stations to the Palace Vendôme. As expected, the shows were no match for the spectacle afforded by the front row: the helmet-headed wives of South American dictators and Arab potentates, toothsome Texas oil heiresses, the frail and vanishing New York Old Guard, the aggressive Seattle New Guard, the Hollywood Couture Curious. I also spotted the venerable fashion eccentric Belladonna Gust at the shows. Belladonna was a British editor who favored hats of immense proportion and convoluted design, and was given to wearing avant-garde dresses made out of mattress ticking and garbage bags—a woman after my own heart, and a true fashion superhero.

I made good on my promise to Billy to cover more than one show by e-mailing him the following show reports.

"Versace: Ribbon-leather dresses. Mermaids. Neptune's Folly."

"Gaultier: Bondage feathers. Mongolian thongs. Emperor's New Clothes."

"La Croix: Clandestine. Immense. Rococo."

"Chanel: De rigueur. Deceit. Duchess of Windsor."

Billy e-mailed back: "Fabooo. Keep it up!" Apparently my succinct reporting had even merited some attention in the fashion press. Already, the Texas bureau of *WWD* had named me the "One-Note Wonder." *Arbiteur*'s website hits were also skyrocketing through the roof, although the site's message board, "Touched by a Model," which asked readers to reveal how models had affected their everyday lives, was still generating the highest numbers. India filled her gossip column with the hanky-panky escapades of naughty moguls with underage enfants and drunken runway models. Billy told us *Arbiteur* had received yet another cease-and-desist letter from Catwalk.com, but it was nothing to worry about. Every night I tucked Boing in over the phone. She was growing so quickly! I wished I had brought her with me, but it seemed cruel to schlep her from show to show in the baby backpack, especially as Bannerjee's back wasn't quite that strong.

I found India saving me a free seat in the front row next to a well-known actress and I marched up to it confidently.

"You'll never guess what I heard," India said.

"What?"

"Teeny's been banned from all the fashion shows this year," she whispered gleefully. "Everyone's talking about it."

"Really?" I gasped.

"Yes, all the fashion designers are incensed at Tart Tarteen. They say she's been stealing all their designs."

"Well, she has," I said.

India nodded. "Apparently they've been getting a lot of flack from their highest-paying customers. Women don't want to see their housecleaners wearing the same outfits that they own, except in chintzy fabrics."

"That is distressing," I agreed, glad that I never found Bannerjee bedecked in head-to-toe Tart Tarteen polyester. "Although it happens every year, anyway, especially right after the Oscars." Personally, I found it quite fun that the same thousand-dollar ball gowns starlets wore on the awards night would soon grace thousands of high school gyms everywhere—the March-into-May syndrome that led directly from the red carpet to the senior prom.

"But I don't think Teeny would miss Couture Week," I said thoughtfully. "It's just not like her to be thwarted so easily."

"Well, I'm going backstage to find out more juicy bits," India said, tottering off. "See you after the show."

I preened and congratulated myself on yet another stolen front-row seat, when I spied Stephan looking bored from across the runway, sitting three rows back. I was pleasantly surprised to see him, especially since Teeny was nowhere to be found.

"Oh, hello there," I called.

His eyes lit up and he smiled broadly, immediately leaving his seat to talk to me.

"We've got to stop meeting like this." I smiled.

"I know," he agreed. "Look at you. You must be a regular customer to get front row."

"Undoubtedly," I said, congratulating myself on keeping up appearances. "So what brings you here? Don't tell me—a friend . . ."

". . . invited me," he finished, and blushed.

"Don't you ever have any work to do?"

He turned a darker shade of crimson. "Well, it's . . ."

"No need to explain," I said. "I was just teasing." If he was as important as Cece had made him out to be—at that Citation Group or whatever—it was common knowledge that the highest-ranking executives at these companies had more than enough time to attend social functions at their whim. Just look at Russell Simmons or Donald Trump. Somehow the daily obligations of running a multibillion-dollar business never put a cramp in their busy social schedules.

"Don't tell me you've turned your hotel room into a camera obscura," I said.

"You remembered."

"Of course," I said. "I think about it all the time."

"Well, I haven't covered my hotel room windows with black curtains if that's what you're asking," he joked. "But it's an idea."

We continued to chat amicably when I was suddenly accosted by a large woman in an ill-fitting peplum suit. "Excuse me, you're not in the right place, this is my seat," she said angrily, flashing her ticket and tapping her foot on the ground impatiently.

Oh no! Now *my* face turned crimson, and I didn't know what to do. The lights had already dimmed and if I gave up my seat, I would probably have to stand in the back with everyone watching and knowing that I had been a front-row impostor—how terribly soul destroying! Stephan gave me a curious look as I began to collect my things, and stood up slowly.

"No—wait," Stephan said, putting a protective hand on my

arm. "I'm sorry, but you must be mistaken," he said, turning to the woman. "This is *definitely* Cat McAllister's seat."

"Cat who?" She was a big-boned Texan who towered over me. "No, I don't think so. This is my seat. You're in *my* seat." She was about to start a ruckus, and several security men walked over to see what the problem was.

"What's going on here?"

"This lady is rudely trying to get herself a front-row seat," Stephan explained, pointing to the pushy Texan. "And this is Cat McAllister; she's a very important editor with *Arbiteur* and undoubtedly one of your biggest customers."

"All right, ma'am, let's go," the security guards said wearily to the Texan. "Sorry about that, we see this all the time."

"I never!" she huffed as the security detail led her out of the show.

I sank back into my seat in relief, looking up at Stephan with adoring eyes. "Thank you," I said. "I don't know how she could get the idea—"

"Listen," he said abruptly. "Do you think you'd like to see Paris upside down and backward with me?"

"I'd love nothing more," I breathed.

"Great. Where are you staying?"

"The Ritz."

"Are you sure?" he joked lightly. "I don't want to get there and find out you've moved."

"No, no. I promise. I'm at the Ritz."

He nodded appreciatively. "Great. I'll meet you there—say at nine o'clock tonight? In the lobby?"

I could only nod happily in reply.

I didn't tell India about my date with Stephan because it seemed more special to keep it to myself for now. She was in the middle of her Ayurvedic exercises, so I left her standing on her head in the middle of the room while I crept downstairs to the lobby to wait for him. I sat down at a lamp-lit table, taking care to position myself on my best side, and noticed Brick Winthrop sitting by himself near the marble fireplace. I caught his eye and gave him a crooked wave of my fashion finger.

Brick left his seat to say hello. "Here to shop as usual?" he asked. "I suppose you've blown every penny?"

"No, I'm actually reporting on the shows this time," I informed him sharply.

"Oh? With *Vogue*?"

"No—with *Arbiteur*."

"Huh. Never heard of it." He shrugged.

I swallowed my irritation. "And you're here with Pasha, I assume? I saw her at Valentino and Givenchy."

"Yes," he harrumphed. "It's even worse here than New York. I can hardly get her alone for an instant. Always some hairstylist or makeup artist or some agency person trailing her wherever she goes." He consulted his watch. "She was supposed to meet me here two hours ago."

I patted his arm supportively. "Well, they are very busy. I know most of the girls are run completely ragged."

His cell phone rang, and he exchanged a few, brief words before snapping it shut in annoyance. "That was her. Apparently she's not going to be able to see me at all. A last-minute fitting for tomorrow. Well, my evening's shot. Care to join me for dinner?"

I explained that I was waiting for Stephan.

"The Westonian?" he snorted. "Well, all right, then. Suit yourself."

When Brick left, I waited . . . and waited . . . and waited. On my fourth glass of champagne I realized I was victim to that most distressing of circumstances that usually afflict either hopelessly dorky nerds or mean-but-popular blond girls in teenage-movie makeover fantasies—I was being stood up. It was not unlike the time when I waited at Grand Central Station for one of my parents to pick me up from summer camp so many years earlier. By the age of seven I was already adept at hailing taxicabs. I would arrive home to an empty penthouse to find Mummy passed out from the party the night before and Daddy still at the office. The housekeeper would express surprise on seeing me at the doorstep and would prepare a lukewarm cup of soup for my dinner. I would eat the soup alone in my room, watching Deney Terrio on *Dance Fever*. When I was little I took all my style cues from *Motion*.

I took the elevator back up to my suite, a frown actually appearing on my forehead regardless of numerous Botox injections.

"What's wrong, darling?" India asked. She had awoken from her nap and was getting ready to go out for the evening.

"Oh, nothing, nothing." I shrugged. "My new shoes are too tight." With my reputation, it was so easy to pan off any apparent discomfort to fashion victimhood.

"I don't know why you don't let your shoemaker stretch them out first," India lectured, helping herself to several bonbons from the hotel's gift basket—she had just discovered Xenical.

"So, what are we going to do tonight?" I asked listlessly. "Why don't we go out?"

I ordered a car. "*Cité auto, s'il vous plaît,*" I said to the concierge. "*Pas de stretch.*"

Les Bains Douches (I wondered why the French hadn't realized they had named a nightclub after Summer's Eve) was a *madhouse.* Naomi, Johnny, Amber, Maddy, Winona, Demi, Elton, Rupert, etc. all aglow. I was lonesome about Stephan and determined to flirt up a storm. Sadly, there was almost no one masculine at the club to flirt with, not counting Donatella, that is. At four in the morning, I departed with two lovely boys from the new Gucci campaign. Why settle for one eye-patch-wearing exiled prince when I could have two chiseled male models? We arrived at my suite in a drunken heap, but once we got in bed all they wanted to do was ransack my closet and try on "outfits." Figures.

The next day I sent the boys away and ordered a yogurt facial. Stephanie Seymour swore by it, and the woman hardly a day over thirty. Oh, India said she was *over* thirty.

Billy called to find out how we were doing. "I miss you girls. The *Arbiteur* fort is lonely."

"Are you doing anything about the cease-and-desist letter from Catwalk.com?" I asked.

"I took the streaming video from New York Fashion Week off the site. That should take care of it."

"OK," I said, but felt doubtful all the same.

I didn't see Stephan at any other show, nor did I see him again in Paris. It was as if he had completely forgotten all about me. On the Concorde back, I couldn't help but notice Teeny in the seat in front of us. She was speaking loudly and excitedly into the air phone.

"Cece, my divorce from Dashiell finally went through!" she was saying. "I know, isn't that fabulous? You do think I can still wear white, don't you? Even for a third wedding?"

There could only be one person she was talking about. Stephan. So that was why I had been stood up. My last shred of hope vanished. Teeny Wong Finklestein Van der Hominie was soon to be *of Westonia!*

18. IPOver

I was inconsolable. The most eligible bachelor in New York was to be just another collectible on Teeny's marital charm bracelet. I wouldn't have cared if it had been anyone else—as far as I was concerned she could have all the eligible bachelors in Manhattan—but Stephan seemed different, a true gentleman and a kindred spirit. He had thought I was funny—hilarious, even. Brick never thought I was funny. I was the one who always had to laugh at *his* jokes.

Nothing helped. Not even fashion. For once my closet didn't inspire me, and living in a renovated campground was getting on my nerves. I missed my princess bed, and the gunnysack I had to wear while inside the apartment was giving me hives.

"Cat, I'm worried about you," India said during a visit to my loft one day soon after we had returned from Paris.

"Why?" I asked, looking up from the wooden plank on the floor, which I hadn't left in days, not even for a shower. Bannerjee had even taken to discreetly opening all the windows and burning scented candles near my corner.

"Is it Stephan? Are you still mooning over him? Forget about him—he stood you up, remember?"

"I know. I know."

"What's that in your hand?" she asked.

"Nothing," I said guiltily, trying to hide it behind my back.

"Give it here," she ordered. I surrendered the roll of raw cookie dough I had been chewing. Since shopping at Barneys only reminded me of Stephan, a ludicrous amount of sugar and fat was the only thing that made me feel better.

"You're really going to have to pull yourself together. Boing misses you terribly. And we have to see about *Arbiteur*. I haven't heard from Billy since we got back, and whenever I buzz his apartment no one answers."

"You're right," I agreed. Heartbreak aside, there were things that needed my attention, and like Olivia Newton-John, who threw her pom-poms at the feet of John Travolta, I wished I'd never laid eyes on that charming, eye-patch-wearing, exiled Westonian rake.

India and I persuaded the supervisor of Billy's building to let us inside the apartment. We grasped each other tightly when we found the office/living room in more disarray than ever. Model look books were torn apart. Clothes samples were strewn everywhere. The floor was littered with invitations, faxes, envelopes, and cigarette butts. India and I exchanged worried glances.

"Billy?" I called tentatively.

"Over here!" a weak voice replied.

India and I made our way to the dining room area, which had once housed the fashion closet. Billy was sitting on a chair and staring at several documents on the table.

"What's wrong, darling?" I asked, reaching out to touch his shoulder.

He handed me the papers then held his head in his hands, making a high-pitched keening sound.

"Oh, no!" I gasped.

"Oh, yes!" India grieved.

The first document was a subpoena from Catwalk.com. They were suing the bejesus out of *Arbiteur,* and we were ordered to appear in court to explain exactly how Catwalk.com's exclusive streaming video of New York Fashion Week had somehow ended up on the *Arbiteur* website. The second letter was from our investment bankers. Apparently they had been alerted to the lawsuit and the prospect of a highly embarrassing legal skirmish meant that under the new circumstances, our impending IPO was to be shelved indefinitely. We were finished. Kaput. My net worth vanished into thin air. With a start I remembered we were all living on borrowed credit—and would have to pay back the money we owed our banker.

"But—but—it doesn't have to be like this. We have insurance against lawsuits, don't we, Billy?" I asked.

"I'm not sure about that," he replied awkwardly.

"What do you mean?"

"I uh, never got around to mailing the insurance forms," he admitted sheepishly. Oooh. I knew exactly what happened, too. After all, the mailbox was *outside* Billy's apartment. Billy only operated within the confines of a door-to-door delivery system—messenger services, Kozmo.com, Federal Express.

"I'm going to have to take down the entire site for a while. I, ah, also have to inform you that our bank has put a hold on our credit line."

India and I slumped against the dining room table. India found an unopened bottle of wine in Billy's refrigerator and poured us each a glass. I passed around cigarettes as a restorative.

"But it gets worse," Billy groaned.

"What, what could be worse than a lawsuit and bankruptcy?" I wailed.

"Jail," Billy whispered.

India and I were stunned.

"No . . ."

"You can't be serious!"

"But how? Why?"

"Oh, both of *you* will be fine. It's me who has to worry."

India and I tried not to look too relieved.

"But why, Billy? Why would you have to go to jail?"

"Because! Because! I'm the one who put that streaming video on our site in the first place! I'm the programmer, remember? I'm the one who broke the law. Stealing streaming video is an intellectual-property offense. Did you know that?"

"Billy, first of all, you're not going to jail," India promised.

"They'll have to take all of us!"

"That's right," I agreed.

"Thanks, girls, but I really don't think that's going to help."

"The worst part of it is that we were just starting to get some attention—we had our best numbers yet, and the *London Telegraph* just dubbed us 'minor celebrities.'"

"Really?" I asked; it wasn't the *New York Observer* 500, but it was a start!

"Recognition at last, now that we have to take down the site," Billy said bitterly.

The next day India and I showed up for work even though there was no need, but we were worried about Billy. The loss of the IPO, the lawsuit from Catwalk.com, and the possibility of incarceration had hit him hard. None of us spoke about the millions of dollars in debt we were in—the subject was too painful. India had canceled her yearly touch-up in Puerto Rico, and it would be a long time before Kozmo.com knocked on Billy's door again. As for the idea that our fearless leader would soon be an inmate of "Oz"—it was too frightening to even consider.

"Well, I've got an idea. It's *Thanksgiving* soon," I said, looking meaningfully at India. "Which means . . ."

"East Hampton," India breathed.

"And more important . . ."

"Mummy!" India and I cheered.

"Mummy?" Billy asked. "What's your mother got to do with it?"

"Oh, she'll find a way out of this mess, you'll see," I said. "Mummy has been in worse scrapes. Plus she's slept with a whole bunch of senators—I'm sure they know all about staying out of jail. She'll be sure to know what to do."

Mummy never missed the annual McAllister Thanksgiving extravaganza, as she was very sentimental when it came to Pilgrims and stuffed turkeys. I sent her another cablegram, hoping this one would reach her at the Kenyan safari, outlining the disaster we found ourselves in. Mummy would come up with something, I just knew she would.

19. thanksgetting and a proposal

In the past, I usually dreaded the imminent trek to southernmost Long Island for the traditional visit, but this year was different. The only drawback to the trip was that it takes absolutely forever to get out of the Five Towns. India's SUV drove wonderfully but Boing threw up in the car all the same. Good girl; she was learning quickly.

"Hello, Cat dear," Grams said as India, Bannerjee, Boing, and I disembarked from the truck.

"India, sweetheart, how are you?" she asked, enfolding India in a bear hug.

"And you remember Bannerjee, my au pair, and that's Boing, my adopted Chinese daughter." I took the baby from Bannerjee's arms and held her out for a kiss.

"Hello, little one," Grams cooed, kissing the air above Boing's forehead. The baby started to bawl and I gave her back to Bannerjee to hold.

"Where's Mummy?" I asked Grams, fully expecting to see Mummy staggering across the lawn with her usual double-fisted cocktails.

"I don't know." Grams shrugged. "Why?"

"But—I sent her a cablegram. I told her it was very important that she spend Thanksgiving with us because I need something. She *never* misses Thanksgiving!"

"Sorry, dear, I haven't heard from her in months."

I slumped. "So she's not here?"

"No, sweetheart. But is there something maybe I could help you with? Are you in some sort of trouble again?"

India nudged me with her elbow, but I was loath to impinge upon my grandmother's goodwill. Grams had already done more than her share of helping me out of sticky financial situations, like paying my bail when I bounced several checks to department stores when I was in college.

"No, it's all right, Grams," I said, while India shot me a disappointed frown.

"I'm sorry your mother couldn't make it. But you know how she is. But anyway, remember that nice boy Brick? He's in the house, he wants to speak to you."

"Really, why?"

"He wouldn't say."

I walked inside the Colonial mansion my father had commissioned to celebrate his short-lived appearance on the Forbes 500 list. My less extravagant grandparents lived in one small wing in the house, which they had modestly furnished to resemble their former home in Jackson Heights. They never did approve of my father's excesses and preferred shag carpeting and Seaman's sectionals to anything Louis Quinze. However, the rest of the house was vintage *Lifestyles of the Rich and Famous*, right down to the gold-encrusted commodes. Brick was waiting for me in the drawing room, which like everything else was done in a frothy Rococo style, with winged cherubs and ornate pink-marble wall treatments.

"Hello, darling," I said coolly.

"Cat," Brick moaned. "I feel awful."

"So do I." I sighed.

Bannerjee, holding Boing, walked through the doorway, and Brick appraised them curiously.

"What's with the baby?" he asked. "Your maid have a kid?"

I was visibly affronted. "No, darling, that's Boing, and, no, she's not Bannerjee's, she's mine."

"*Boing?* What kind of name is that for a baby?" he asked. "Boing. It sounds like a doorbell. Or a cartoon. *Boing, boing, boing.*"

"It's an ancient Chinese name," I said defensively. "It's distinctive."

"Well, it's just . . . stupid. Why'd you have to go and do that for, anyway?" he asked, peevish and annoyed.

"Do what?"

"You know what I'm talking about," he snapped, meaning the international cross-racial adoption. "Anyway, I wanted to tell you. She's left me." He groaned.

"Who?" I asked, knowing full well who. I just wanted to hear him say it for the satisfaction.

"Pasha," he gurgled.

"Oh. Why?"

"For a gangsta rapper," he sobbed. "Some foul-mouthed nineteen-year-old with a few number-one hit singles on the *Billboard* charts." And the bestselling album of the year, I thought to myself.

"I'm sorry, darling," I soothed. "It will be all right. There will be other Victoria's Secret supermodels." Poor thing. Didn't he know he was just the latest casualty on the seraphic Soviet supermodel's dance card? Her first boyfriend was her photo agent, and she had quickly traded him in for the president of her modeling agency, but then left him for Brick, the billionaire. Unfortunately for Brick, all the money in the world couldn't compete with the status of a gangbanging white rapper. It was certain Pasha wouldn't be left outside of any fabulous parties in the future.

"I don't want any more supermodels. I'm finished with them."

"You are?"

"Yes." He nodded. Brick looked glassily into my eyes. "I've had enough. I want you."

"Me?" I yelped.

"You. You'd never leave me for a ridiculously pompous gang banger, would you? Some roughneck from Detroit? You detest gangsta rap."

"Well . . . I suppose I do. . . ." My tastes did run toward Goth, New Wave, and bubble-gum pop but I didn't see what that had to do with anything.

"Cat . . . will you marry me?" Brick asked suddenly.

"Marry you?"

"Yes."

"Yes," I repeated.

"Great!"

"No. I mean, why? It's not like you haven't asked me before," I said. "Remember? Brick, we've been engaged more times than I can count."

"I know, I know, but I've changed. I promise. Really," he wheedled. "There just comes a time when I should settle down, you know?"

"I see." I pushed Brick's bangs out of his eyes. "Oh, darling—let me think about it."

"All right." He sighed. "Well, let me know soon. I should be getting back. I'm entertaining a very special guest," he said mysteriously.

The next afternoon during a brisk sail, I finally confessed to India that Brick had reproposed.

"Well, that's fabulous," India said. "This time, get him to the altar quickly instead of just putzing around like you did before."

"I know. I suppose it's what I want. And the Winthrops have one of the best family crests—his grandfather commissioned an artist to make one in 1926."

"And think about it. With Brick's gazillions, he'll help defend *Arbiteur* from the Catwalk.com lawsuit for sure," India added.

"For sure," I agreed. I was sure once I told Brick about the legal problems of the website, he would offer the services of his ace legal team to help us out and keep Billy out of jail—providing I agreed to marry him, of course.

India and I gazed out into the distance, musing on the new turn of events.

"Oh, look, there he is now!"

Brick was out on his sailboat, and I got a glimpse of his special guests—and oh my Lord, it was none other than England's Prince William himself! We waved to Brick and the bonnie prince. Bannerjee was beside herself, and was a particularly enthusiastic waver. In her frenzy she toppled overboard, landing near Brick's boat. Prince William was such a gentleman, he actually fished her out of the water. 'Bye, Banny!

Thanksgiving dinner was unremarkable, with relatives nodding off from predinner cocktails before Gramps had even carved Grams's undercooked turkey. I repaired to my childhood room to spend a quiet evening playing Scrabble with Boing. She can't seem to spell anything yet so I won easily! Hard to believe Boing still hasn't learned English. After all, she watches the Teletubbies every day. When the baby nodded off, I tucked her in her crib and knocked on India's door.

"Yesss?"

"Darling, it's me. Can I come in?" I asked.

"Mmmmrrrmmph."

I let myself inside and sat on the edge of her bed. "India, darling, I'm going absolutely batty here. Do get up. I'm so tense I can't think straight," I said crossly.

"Do you have anything? I asked meaningfully.

"Hmm, let's see what I can do. After all, this *is* the Hamptons."

*   *   *

India came through and procured some fun for us, finally. Nice stuff if you can get it. That India! She could spot the nearest dealer anywhere! I unwrapped the little square of tinfoil and looked happily at the white powder inside. Now, I was never much of a druggie—one of my biggest regrets, actually, since as Drew Barrymore has proven, it's rehab that's glamorous. But pot was a fat girl's drug, Ecstasy made me nauseous, and as for heroin—well, I've seen *Trainspotting*. Plus, I dabbled so rarely it was almost embarrassing.

I cut it up into nice little white lines. India rolled a dollar bill and passed it over. We each took a monster snort. Bleccch. It stung.

"Hmmm . . . do you feel anything?" India asked.

"No, do you?"

"No," she lamented.

We waited for a while for something to kick in.

"It's not working! We've been robbed!" I anguished.

India dipped a finger in the white powder and tasted it. "This isn't cocaine at all!"

"And I'm *allergic* to baking soda!" I complained.

Even so, we decided to snort it anyway on the off chance that it was something deliciously illegal, and fifteen minutes later, I was overwhelmed by a desire to do something—*anything*—I was frantic—couldn't sit still—finally I realized I could do one thing—I could straighten up the room—I could clean—I could—I could *vacuum*!

"Where on earth does Grams keep the Hoover?"

India and I had returned from the vet's. During my baking soda buzz, I had accidentally vacuumed Miu Miu, who had come to the Hamptons with us, right up. Ooops! Didn't know if India would ever forgive me. "How would you feel if I did the same to Boing?" she accused me. Well, since she put it that way . . . Funeral plans for Miu Miu were postponed until India recuperated. We arrived back at the compound to find Bannerjee sitting glumly by the gates.

"Banny, you're back so soon?" I asked.

"By Her Majesty's Secret Service," a ruddy-faced bodyguard told us, appearing from the shadows. He saluted and left. I never did find out what had conspired between my Sri Lankan au pair and the prince. Nevertheless, Fleet Street tabloids were somehow tipped off that William had fallen for an "Indian princess." Upon hearing the shocking news, his actual girlfriend, a proper English blueblood, promptly lost her mind, her virginity, and her chance at the throne. As for Bannerjee, I was just glad she was spared a gruesome death on a lonesome Parisian highway.

"So, have you given it any more thought?" Brick asked the day we were preparing to return to the city.

"I have," I told him.

"And?"

"I'm sorry, Brick, but I can't. I don't feel right about it anymore." Our relationship used to be enough for me—and I knew that if we were married, my life would be so much easier. God knows I would never have had to worry about money ever again. Plus, even if Brick didn't have short blond hair and a way with killer rhymes or command masses of hysterical screaming fans or live a life of lavish degeneration, he could always be counted on for a good table at Alain Ducasse, at least. But if I accepted his proposal, we would be back to our old routine: he would always be off somewhere, either climbing Mount Kilimanjaro or else backpacking in Borneo, and I'd have little to look forward to other than an endless round of speakerphone-tag. I already sent unanswered cablegrams to my mother, I didn't want to live the rest of my life fielding long-distance phone calls from my husband.

"Is there someone else?" he asked finally.

"No, there isn't," I said flatly, thinking of Teeny cooing about her third wedding dress.

On the drive back to Manhattan, I explained my decision to India. Ever steadfast, she assured me she understood. "That's fine. We'll find some other way," she said, trying not to sound too hopeless. And then she said, slowly, "You know what, there *is* another way."

"What?"

"The annual MogulFest in Sun Valley, Idaho!"

"Come again?"

"You know, the annual meeting of billionaires and CEOs and media moguls that's all very hush-hush and secret? Where they all dance naked in the woods and stuff?"

"Oh, yes, I remember. Brick used to be very secretive about that. He went every year."

"Well, when we won the Nettie Award, Billy mentioned that we got an automatic invitation to go as minimoguls."

"But we don't have a website anymore," I chided. "Remember?"

"That's why we have to go. We're bound to find an investor willing to take a chance and finance us there. Sun Valley is very technofriendly. Plus, they won't care that we're being sued—I mean, look at Microsoft."

20. surviving sun valley

Traveling via commercial airlines is incredibly unglamorous, so it was fortunate that India and I were able to hitch a last-minute ride aboard a generous billionaire's Gulfstream jet. The other passengers included several long-term members of the conference, emeritus directors like Bill Gates, as well as active members like Larry Ellison, Ingrid Casares, David Geffen, Calvin Klein, Donna and Madonna, Barbra Streisand, Robs Redford and Reiner, the dueling gemstones Jewel and Bijoux, as well as Tina, Calista, and Ivana. We were set for an invigorating weekend where the whole privileged lot of us would determine the course of global culture for the millennium. I only hoped India and I were up to the task! Billy had approved of the plan and wished us the best of luck finding an investor.

Sitting in the lap of luxury fifty thousand feet in the air, I reveled in the plush carpeting, private televisions with 235 cable channels, Barcaloungers, top-shelf spirits, and catered food from New York's top chefs. I myself popped a Tic Tac and ordered a vodka tonic. Jeff Bezos passed by and waved hello; India and I corralled him before anyone else could and floated the possibility of Amazon acquiring *Arbiteur.* "Think of it—Arbazon.com," I suggested.

"We'll talk, Jeffy darling," India promised.

"Have your people call my people."

I loved saying that line even though *Arbiteur*'s "people" was our one disheveled CEO in a ratty tank top. Billy also served as *Arbiteur*'s secretary when that was called for, answering the phone in the patently fake British accent essential to running a fashion business. But we never did hear from Jeff Bezos.

I prepared to settle into a sweet slumber, my head resting on India's shoulder, when I heard the now-too-familiar screech.

"CAT!!!"

I opened one eye, but I already knew who it was. Only one woman could burn rubber and break glass with the sound of her high-pitched voice.

"Hi, Teeny."

"What on earth are you doing here?" she tittered, perching on my armrest. "Oh, wait—don't tell me. You're on your way to the new Sun Valley Canyon Ranch."

"No, *Arbiteur* won the Nettie Award for best fashion website. The winner gets an automatic invite to MogulFest," I sniffed.

"Oh, right," she said blankly. "What's *Arbiteur* again? Oh, that *little* website. What is it you do for them?"

"For your information, I wrote all the show reviews this season."

"Show reviews? *Arbiteur* actually gets tickets to the fashion shows?"

"Well, standing-room tickets mostly," I conceded, blushing. "But, yes, we are an accredited fashion media outlet."

"How nice for you. Listen, if you need any help getting around or meeting people, just ask me, I've been to this *lots* of times. I remember so many crazy times—like when we locked up Uncle Morty, that's Steven Spielberg to you, in the outhouse as a dare—oh, he loved that . . ." She giggled. "Hold on, there's Ralph Lauren. Excuse me, I've got to say hi." Teeny bounded over to her next victim.

When she left, I spotted Stephan seated in the next row. I should have known he would be at MogulFest! Especially since Teeny was here too. My heart leapt and our eyes met for the briefest of moments, but I quickly looked away, determined to banish him from my psyche.

"Cat!" he said happily, giving me a cheerful wave.

I ignored the wounded look on his face when I didn't return his greeting, as I had absolutely nothing to say to a man who had the audacity to stand me up for a date and then never even contact me to apologize. With fierce intensity I perused the agenda for this year's meeting, which included a slew of trust-building games wherein we would guide blindfolded team members to hike mountains, cross whitewater rapids, rope-walk across gorges, and have sex with Harvey Keitel. Eek!

Four hours later, the plane landed in a deserted airfield, and a fleet of stretch limousines arrived to take us to our cabins.

"I love the country air!" a telecommunications billionaire said, taking a strong whiff.

"It's good to be back!" the CEO of a powerful television network marveled, lowering himself into a deep knee bend.

"Will you look at those mountains!" a retired information specialist and the new owner of a franchise basketball team enthused.

"Hmmm," I said, slapping my forearm where a bug had landed. "Where's the nearest bar?"

India and I settled into our well-heated cabin and exchanged air kisses with our bunkmates, high-profile members of the Velvet Mafia—a twenty-something hunky matinee idol and a fifty-something big-cheese movie producer. We really lucked out, as they were being more than sweet and had stocked the bathroom with the best bath products!

"So, what do you think?" I asked India when we were tucked in for the night. She had taken the bottom bunk. "Do you think we have any prospects?"

"Mmm . . . Oh, definitely," she said, meaning several of the CEOs were partial to women of the transsexual variety.

"No, I mean for *Arbiteur*, silly."

"Oh, right." India thought for a moment. "None."

"Well, we might as well make the most of this conference," I said. "Why don't you take 'How to Conquer the World Through Your Operating System,' and I'll go to 'The Justice Department: Necessary Evil or Evil Empire?' and then we can meet at lunch for Martha Stewart's 'Living Like a Billionaire Is the Best Revenge Marathon.'"

"All right," India agreed. "But I don't want to miss 'Ivana: The Early Years.'"

The next day I attended a Post-Stress-Relaxation-and-Conquest seminar led by a handsome Indian guru who taught us how to channel creative and spiritual energy to conquer the world through marketing, self-promotion, and slavish celebrity endorsements to induce a frenzy of mass consumption. I spotted Teeny scribbling furiously on her Palm Pilot. Other seminars included "QVC versus the Home Shopping Network," "Extracting the V Chip," "Web-TV Convergence: Are a Million Channels the Wave of the Future?" "How to Divorce Your Fifth Wife Without Paying Alimony," and "Advanced Class in Matching Denim Shirts with Chino Pants."

All along, I alternatively hoped and feared that I would bump into Stephan. I assumed he was bunking with Teeny on the other side of the hill, and I looked for him in all my seminars but so far, no such luck. Which was just as well, considering. Besides, I had more than enough to keep myself busy, as between mogul bonding there were volleyball games, touch football, and goat rodeo. Of course, the retreat wasn't just all work and no play. A tasteful but star-studded celebration has been planned. There would be singing around the campfire with Limp Bizkit, gourmet marshmallows from the south of France, a laser light show followed by a private fireworks display, and an authentic hoedown with the Dixie Chicks in the resort ballroom.

During the party, I shared corndogs with Mark Andreesen and Geraldine Laybourne by the campfire.

"It's a new fashion website and we just won the Nettie Award for best fashion site," I explained. "We're really growing by leaps and bounds. Our readership includes the most fashion-addicted people on the planet. It's an extremely savvy group."

I babbled on about our cost-effective production ethics, our low overhead, our growing recognition and acclaim. "We've been reviewed by the *South China Post* and *Saudi Arabia Today!*" I was so immersed in conversation I didn't even notice that someone had joined the edge of our group and was listening to everything I said.

During the final night's hoedown, I do-si-doed with a corpulent telecommunications magnate and twirled him over to India, who was sitting by herself in the corner inhaling marshmallows. She should be careful, I thought, even with Xenical, if she didn't look out she'd have major FOP: fat over platforms. I left the two of them to finish the dance and called home to find out how Bannerjee and Boing were holding up.

"Banny darling! How are you?"

"Mmmff?" Bannerjee mumbled into the phone.

"HOW ARE YOU!" I yelled again.

"Fffpppfff Mxsadfadsdaf."

"Banny, I can't hear you? Is someone there?" I asked. In the background was the unmistakable sound of loud music blaring and snippets of conversation in . . . hmm . . . was that Norwegian-accented English? "Dutte, this direct TV rocks out, man!" "Banny, where is Cristal?" and even, "Duuutte, I've gotta get back to the club, I work door tonight."

"Oh, is nothing, Miss Cat, the television is on," Bannerjee assured me when the static had cleared. Tired of watching television through a pair of binoculars, especially since our neighbor seemed to have a fondness for boring nature shows on the Discovery Channel, I had a new satellite dish installed so Boing could watch Cantonese soap operas. It would help her understand where she came from.

"Let me talk to the baby," I said. "Why don't you put her on the line?"

"Huh? Oh, yes, um, just wait a minute—"

And the line went dead.

I tried calling again but this time there was no answer. Strange. I berated myself for leaving the two of them alone, what with the stalker milling around. I had told Heidi to call him off, but she told me she had no idea what I was talking about.

Dear Lord, what if there really was an evil man who was keeping track of all my actions? I had a flash of anxiety as I morbidly fantasized what would happen if Boing were kidnapped in my absence. Would she be found, ten years later, living in a shack upstate and thinking herself to be just another ordinary hick, not knowing her true, fabulous identity? Would she then publish a book, *I Know My Name Is Boing*? Would I be given my own network television show, *America's Most Hunted*? What about film rights—who would play me in the heart-wrenching story of my adopted baby daughter's disappearance? (Michelle Pfeiffer? Jessica Lange?)

I tried to shrug off my fears and rejoined the party to rescue the red-faced telecommunications mogul from India's clutches.

"That's the ticket! That's the ticket!" India encouraged him as the old codger twirled her around and around so that she looked like a multicolored Mexican piñata.

Finally, it was our last day at the retreat. I, for one, was glad to be done with all this consensus building, strategic partnership, and cultural-dissemination thingamajig. Plus, I hadn't been able to shop in three days! I was suffering from Barneys withdrawal. Unlike Aspen, there were no off-road designer boutiques in Sun Valley. I found the next best thing and ravaged the neighboring Native American reservation for something, anything, to buy, and picked up some choice feather headdresses to go with my resort-collection Gallianos.

"'Bye, darlings," I told the movie hunk and big-cheese producer when we were packed and ready to depart. "Shanti-Astangi to you both!"

"As-Salaamu'Alaykum." They nodded.

The same stretch limousines returned us to the airfield, but when we arrived to board the plane, we were stopped by the pilot, who met us in front of the landing strip.

"We're not going to be able to take off!" he told us. "There's no radio contact from Los Angeles or New York! I can't bring up the tower!"

We gasped. It was all fine to drink in the country air and the beauty of the Idaho mountains for a weekend—but not for one second more. The moguls and entertainers and CEOs around us attempted to find out what was happening, punching in numbers on their cell phones and booting up wireless Internet connections on their Palm Pilots, but it was useless. Finally, the chief of the Native American reservation came out to explain what had happened. He had picked up the news from sending a cloud to his cousin in the Hudson River Valley.

Apparently a crippling computer virus had devastated the world's electronic system in forty-eight hours, garnering it the nickname "the Hong Kong flu." Forwarding itself through international e-mailboxes, it had instantly grounded planes, short-circuited ATM machines, blown out satellites (no cell phones, faxes, computers, Palm Pilots, Genies, beepers, television, cable, nothing!), and had left the entire country in a blackout. The looting and rioting had begun in the major metropolitan areas and the National Guard had been dispatched to restore peace, giving them a break from disarming children in the Midwest. I'd never seen so many billionaires look so gloomy since the AOL Time Warner merger. We were ferried back to the resort, which was empty as all the staff had already been sent home. It looked like we'd have to take care of ourselves.

Several of the assembled guests didn't take to the news too well—after all, it was one thing to be invited to a swank Adventureland escape, where helpful outdoor counselors rounded up the walleyes for you to spearfish in the shallows, but quite another to realize that we were trapped in a remote mountain hideaway with only our nonworking electronic equipment to keep us company. Where was Tom Hanks when you needed him? Several of the moguls took the news stoically and quickly shifted into leadership mode, organizing the assembled into tribes: hunters, gatherers, and whiners.

I turned to India and our two bunkmates.

"Here, try this," the big-cheese movie producer said to his hunky movie star boyfriend as he handed him his cell phone.

The hunky movie star then rubbed the cell phone and the Palm Pilot together in an attempt to ignite a spark and light a fire.

"Oh, good Lord, let me do it," India huffed. "Cat, take off your shoes."

I took off my Blahniks with a worried look on my face. "What are you doing?"

"Pish-pish," India dismissed me, as she took my shoes and rubbed them together. Slowly, smoke began to form.

"Wooden heels," India explained.

I was traumatized at the loss of my shoes, but glad to have the warmth of the campfire. My thoughts then turned to Banny and Boing back home. I hoped they were all right in New York.

As the days progressed, we learned to survive through ancient techniques taught to us by Chief Speeding Jet and from our collective memories of *Survivor*. We subsisted on corncakes and yams, and smoke signal junkies were limited to five clouds a day. In the evenings, we sat around the campfire telling horror stories about badly executed takeovers and 100 percent stock dives. I even became a full-fledged member of the Native American tribe. My beaded Swarovski necklace came in *über*-handy. I was now the proud owner of Manhattan.

"Cat! Cat! Look up in the sky!" India exclaimed one afternoon as we harvested corn from the fields.

"What is it?"

"It's an airplane! We're saved! They've fixed the computer virus!"

"Oh, thank God!" I said. "I'd kill for an air conditioner right now!"

I went back to my cabin to pack up, when I saw Stephan headed my way, looking weary and fatigued.

"Oh, hi," I said, affecting an air of insouciance.

"Cat," he said with relief. "I've been looking for you everywhere."

"Really? Why?"

"I wanted to apologize. For Paris. I would have liked to apologize earlier but you're still unlisted. So I thought I'd find you through *Arbiteur,* but even that number's been disconnected."

I flushed. "So?"

"Well, I just wanted to explain why I didn't see you that night. I did go to the lobby of the Ritz, to meet you. But when I arrived I saw you with Brick Winthrop and I just thought . . . well." He shook his head. "Cece always told me you were still pining for him. So I thought you were playing a game or something. Saying you'll meet me for dinner but then meeting your ex-boyfriend instead."

"But Brick and I were just talking . . . it was nothing."

"It was?"

"Yes. Of course. But what about you?" I asked.

"What about me?"

"Aren't you—aren't you engaged to Teeny?"

"To Teeny?" He laughed out loud. "No, of course not!"

"So you're not going to marry her?"

"Marry her? Where on earth did you get that idea?"

"But you—you took her to my birthday party. I mean, that party at that club—where she blew out the candles."

"For some reason she really wanted to go to that party. She was a friend of Cece's so I obliged. It was a favor."

"And I saw you having lunch with her downtown."

"You did? Why didn't you say hello?"

I shrugged helplessly. "I don't know. And in Paris I assumed . . . you're really not with Teeny?"

Stephan grimaced. "No. I told you, she's just a friend," he said impatiently.

"But Cece said—"

"Cece, it appears, says a lot of things," he said wisely. "She told me you were still in love with Brick."

"But I'm not," I protested.

"No, you're not. But funnily enough, Teeny is."

"Teeny's in love with Brick?" I gaped.

"Yes, that's all she talks about, actually. It's why she wanted to go to your birthday party—she thought Brick would be there."

A dim memory of Teeny throwing herself at Brick during our engagement party several years before entered my mind. I was so used to Teeny wanting exactly what I wanted that it never occurred to me that she was still fixated on my old flame. And come to think of it, the night she had introduced him to Pasha, the Slavic super-model, Teeny had looked just as furious as I had when Brick left the party with her.

"Listen, Cat, I'm only in Sun Valley because I wanted to see you again."

"Really? Why?"

"Because I'm, uh, quite taken with you, if you haven't noticed." He coughed.

Oh. Oh. Oh.

We had that long-awaited kiss. Delirious. Delicious. Much better than I had anticipated. This was it! Who would have thought? The handsome eye-patch-wearing Westonian prince—mine! Lights—camera—comeback! I *knew* I would soon be joining that great committee meeting in the sky—I mean, at the Costume Institute.

* PART THREE *

kingdom come

21. castles in the air

Stephan proposed on bended knee, and I immediately accepted, of course. We went back to MogulFest to pack our bags and to share the good news with India.

"Darling, that's wonderful!" she cheered, enveloping me in a giant bear hug. "Congratulations!"

"I know!" I cheered back. "I'm going to be a princess!"

"Of Westonia!"

"Not even a last name—just a country!"

India dropped me a demure curtsey. It was just like in that scene in that television movie of the week where Catherine Oxenberg played you-know-who and her "flatmates" all bowed down to her. I was touched.

On the plane ride back to civilization I daydreamed about the perfect wedding: the whole grand striped-tent, American-roses, white-glove affair that entailed the services of the Peter Duchin Orchestra and a much-anticipated trip to Vera Wang's cozy boutique. Or perhaps I could go the downtown route: wedding as "happening." Like Vanessa Beecroft's, it would be a memorable frisson and fusion of avant garde and Old Guard. Three words: White. Plastic. Versace. A minidress and thigh-high white patent-leather boots. We would exchange vows in a loft, overlooking the city skyline, as the Gay Men's Chorus sang Bette Midler and Edith Piaf tunes. A disco ball and drag queen attendants—what better way to cross the threshold than with India by my side. Guests would include Happy Rockefeller next to Li'l Kim next to Norman Mailer. It would be glorious!

But of course there was only one dead celebrity whose wedding dress I could wear for the most important day of my life—yes, the dead celebrity of all dead celebrities! Princess Diana's wedding dress. Thank God I had had the foresight to buy it on eBay years ago!

I looked down at Stephan, slumbering against my shoulder, and wondered if he owned a military dress uniform from Westonia.

And with Stephan's riches, he would secure funding for *Arbiteur*; oh, it was too perfect.

Back in Manhattan, Stephan and I drove right from the airport to Harry Winston. While his proposal was as romantic as I could have hoped, there was still the matter of *the ring*.

"What about this one?" I asked, pointing to a fifteen-carat wonder that could obliterate the sun. "I know, I could ask them to put it aside and you can surprise me with it!" I said breathlessly.

"Mmm . . ."

Stephan suggested he move in with me immediately, and I didn't see why not. "Don't you need anything from your apartment?" I asked, seeing that he only had a backpack with him from the trip.

"No, I don't really need much," he said.

"Oh."

When we arrived at the loft, he was taken aback at the sight of the exposed wooden beams, the electrical cords hanging from the ceilings, as well as the lack of furniture. "What's all this?" he asked, looking around curiously at the Lechters coolers and the wooden planks.

"Home, darling! *Nouveau* minimalism." I explained, confused at finding the floor littered with cigarette ashes, empty champagne bottles, and invitations to nightclubs hosted by Norwegian party promoters.

He surveyed the premises and put down his backpack next to the temperature-controlled closet. "When you said you were a minimalist, I didn't quite expect it to be so . . . sparse."

Motioning to the exposed shower, he asked doubtfully, "You live in the bathroom?"

Hmmm . . . I supposed I'd have to ask Brother Parish to do something about that now that we had a man in the house.

"Well, I know it's not much," I said, gazing out at the empty expanse. "But of course we don't have to stay here all the time." I thought dreamily of his Fifth Avenue apartment and international real estate acquisitions. Baden-Baden, Beverly Hills, Buenos Aires . . .

"Of course not," Stephan agreed, his face lighting up.

I raced around, calling for Bannerjee —I couldn't wait to show Boing to Stephan, I knew he would love her immediately. I found Bannerjee tending to Boing, who was sleeping peacefully on her duvet coat. Thank heavens they were both all right! Banny giggled when I introduced her to Stephan.

"Oh, Banny, I'm so glad you and the baby made it through the great computer virus blackout!"

"What blackout?" Bannerjee asked. Apparently, the Hong Kong flu had done little to change life at our bare-bones homestead.

"You know, the one that short-circuited all the world's computers and caused an electric shortage."

"Ah, that why satellite television stop working," Banny mused. "I think you forget pay cable bill."

I picked up the sleeping baby and handed her to Stephan.

"She's beautiful," Stephan marveled. Boing opened her eyes

groggily and reached up and grabbed his finger with her entire hand.

I watched the two of them together, my heart melting.

With Stephan at my side, we were bound to become one of those Manhattan couples who instantly added a cachet to any event, whose bliss-filled lives were assiduously documented step-by-step in glossy, oversize pages of very important magazines.

My first phone call was from Cece Phipps-Langley herself.

"Darling, is it true?"

"Is what true?"

"That you and Stephan are engaged? I saw India at the hair salon, she told me."

"Yes, it is very true."

"Well, you do have my heartfelt congratulations," she purred. "Tell me, would you and Stephan be available for a little get-together I'm throwing next week? I'm hosting a dinner for Brooke Astor."

"Of course, darling," I cooed.

Once Cece spread the word, my phone was ringing off the hook with luncheon invitations, private dinner parties, and junior committee chairwomen beseeching me to join their planning committees. I had my pick of a litter of diseases and global catastrophes and philanthropic art projects.

Since it was well known that Stephan was related to all the royal houses in Europe, New York society was beside itself with the rumor that the queen herself would be in attendance at our nuptials. The clamoring for invitations to the wedding caused the fax machine to spit out numerous entreaties from one Manhattan hostess after another—it was worse than the frenzy for reservations at a newly crowned four-star restaurant.

And who was I to keep the news from a fawning public? I was sure the press would go absolutely wild once they were appraised of our engagement. Everyone loves a princess. I'd have Heidi schedule interviews with Diane Sawyer, Barbara Walters, and Howard Stern. I was certain to be inundated with requests for numerous puffy profiles. I had my heart set on every glossy magazine's style section: "In Her Closet" for *Harper's Bazaar*, "Celebrity Closet Case" for *Vogue*; maybe there would even be cover stories in *Town & Country* and *Manhattan File*; perhaps Stephan and I would be caricatured in the front fold of the "Observatory" section of the *New York Observer*. And to think, what if *The New York Times* sent a lifestyle reporter to spend an hour shopping with me! "At Barneys with Cat McAllister," I imagined the headline reading.

"What do you think?" I asked Stephan when I told him about my plans for a burgeoning media tidal wave.

"It's great," he agreed weakly. "But don't you think a more private wedding would be in order?"

Privacy? Pish-posh. Besides, I had already commissioned Sergio, the mastermind behind several of the most famous weddings in recent history. The one who had chosen Carolyn Bessette-Kennedy's nightgown-style wedding dress, alerted the helicopters to Madonna and Sean Penn's nuptials, and convinced Tommy and Pamela to renew their vows in the nude. Who knew what he would have in mind for our wedding! A Blue Angel salute while Whitney Houston forgot the words to "I Will Always Love You"?

The next day I returned to Harry Winston only to find that Stephan had yet to purchase the fifteen-carat rock I'd picked out the day before. What was taking him so long? I drummed my fingers on the glass display case in annoyance.

"What's the matter? No diamond big enough for you?" a voice asked.

I looked up to see Brick smirking at me.

"Oh, hi, darling."

"Congratulations on your engagement, by the way," Brick said.

"Why, thank you," I said politely.

"I just wanted to say you've chosen the right man."

"That's good of you to say."

"But you know, I just wanted to tell you that I finally remembered where I've met your Stephan before."

"Oh? Where?"

"At Barneys."

"Well, that's a funny coincidence." I laughed. "That's where I first met him too."

"I mean, *at* Barneys. He's a tailor at Barneys."

"What?"

"He works for Barneys. And not at the executive offices either, believe me. He fitted me for a bespoke suit not too long ago," he explained with a wide grin.

"Brick, I don't know what kind of sick joke you're playing here . . ."

Brick chuckled. "Prince of Westonia, my ass. He's my tailor at Barneys. Ask him yourself."

"I will!" I threatened, stomping off the elevator in a rage. I decided Brick really needed to take some medication. Demerol deficiency was certainly not a laughing matter.

22. alien abduction

Stephan a tailor at Barneys? How could it be true? Why, it was Cece Phipps-Langley herself who told me Stephan was rich and single and titled, and Cece's word was as good as . . . well . . .

On second thought I remembered how often Cece was taken in by silver-tongued social climbers boasting ersatz elite backgrounds. There was the beautiful boy who claimed to be Steven Spielberg's nephew and a friend of her son's at prep school. He looked nothing like Steven Spielberg, and, indeed, turned out to be a Pakistani teenager whose real name was Anoushivran Fakhran. And what about her other pet project, Alberto de van Mije, the international playboy who passed himself off as a Cuban count—even though Cuba doesn't and has never had an aristocracy?

How many times have I heard stories about this person or that person claiming to be from Geneva or East Egg or Locust Valley who turned out to be nothing more than ambitious art history students from New Jersey who had read Diane von Furstenberg's autobiography as a shortcut to dropping hints of childhoods in Cologne and finishing schools in Switzerland? New York was the kind of place where you could reinvent yourself all the way up to noshing with the de Ocampos and the de la Rentas at Le Cirque. All you needed was a funny accent, a good haircut, and a great wardrobe. Gulp. Stephan certainly had all three. But it was such an awful thought, I couldn't finish it.

Billy had called an emergency meeting and I arrived at *Arbiteur* to find him galvanized and the office tidied up just the tiniest bit—the new beauty product samples had all been put away into his medicine cabinet.

"What's going on?" I asked.

India, who was sitting in her usual place, on the armrest, shrugged.

"Well, girls, it looks like MogulFest worked out after all," Billy said grimly.

"How so?"

"We have a buyer."

"We do?"

"Somebody is willing to buy *Arbiteur*?"

"Yes."

"Who?"

"They wouldn't say. But their lawyers contacted me on the day you both were leaving from MogulFest. Apparently they took a meeting with you at the conference."

"They did?" I asked, racking my brains to remember if we had actually met anyone who had expressed an interest in buying *Arbiteur*. India looked just as confused as I did. As far as I remembered, we didn't really do a lot of networking in Sun Valley.

"And they've assured me they have a way to take care of the Catwalk.com lawsuit," he said slowly.

"So that's great!" India cheered.

"Isn't it?" I asked Billy.

"But there's a catch."

"Of course there is. What is it?"

"They want editorial control."

"Why?"

"They're an apparel company, and they want to use our editorials to influence our audience of extreme fashion addicts."

"Sounds shady," India noted.

"And they're only offering one million dollars to buy the entire company."

"One million dollars! That's an insult!" India cried. "We're worth a thousand times more than that! We're an Internet company!"

"I know." Billy sighed. "But they know about the imaginary staff, and the truth about the number of impressions we serve a day."

"How horrible!"

"They're willing to keep Cat and me on as editors, on a good salary . . . but—" he said, turning to India.

"But?"

"But there's one catch—India."

"Me?" India gulped.

"They don't want you to be part of the new *Arbiteur*."

"Why not?" I demanded.

"They think *'Depeche Merde'* is a liability. They don't like how India makes fun of celebrities."

"Well, I never!" India was so insulted for once she had nothing to say for the moment. Then she looked at the two of us and told us in a quavering voice, "That's fine, darlings. I have lived through worse. Don't worry about me."

Poor India. It wasn't the first time she had found herself in dire straits. I remembered how a few years earlier, when we had met up again in New York after losing touch after Japan, she had shown up at my doorstep, a chubby, puffy wreck with brittle hair and a disgraceful manicure, wearing a shabby, yellow-stained Pucci sheath that hugged in all the wrong places, giving the impression of psychedelic sausage casing.

Apparently after coasting the New Wave tsunami for a while,

India's short-lived foray into Jap-and-roll ended abruptly in 1985, when the New Kids on the Block burst on the international music scene. Suddenly, the Japanese who used to be mad for sloe-eyed, ambiguously sexual, ersatz British rock stars went crazy over apple-cheeked Boston pseudotoughs. India's band could barely land a gig, and she was not about to part with the lip liner and asymmetric haircut for a Chess King wardrobe. So the band fired India, who then drifted from one louche assignment to another, answering phones at an upper-class whorehouse one day, cleaning toilets in a gay bathhouse the next.

India didn't know what to do, but certainly wasn't content with just wearing sissy-boy clothes anymore. India wanted the real thing—to reveal her true nature and unleash it upon an innocent world. India was ready to be India. But the process turned out to be more expensive than she anticipated, too much even for a boy of her quasi-aristocratic blood—not that her family's crumbling estate in Normandy was worth anything. But somehow, she lied, cheated, and wormed her way into a bit of money and repaired posthaste to Denmark for the life-changing procedure.

Unfortunately after several weeks, India was still sporting a concave chest, facial hair, and a voice as deep as a ravine. India needed more work: more surgery, more hormone therapy, not to mention a much more fabulous wardrobe. Why become a woman if the closest she could get was Billy Jean King's ugly older sister? India was in danger of living life as a failed transsexual, if there was ever such a thing.

I took her in, of course; hanging around her tiny studio apartment decorated with Patrick Nagel posters, lip-synching to whatever Culture Club or Flock of Seagulls cover she was going to perform that night, were some of the happiest, most carefree times of my life. So, as per the suggestion of an imperious transvestite we met at a Tupperware party at the Gay and Lesbian Center on Christopher Street, I took India to Puerto Rico to get it done correctly. In the homeland of Menudo, India became a woman at last. The full-body liposuction was a birthday gift.

I was there for her then, and there was no way I would let her down now.

"It's not *Arbiteur* without India."

"Of course not," Billy said.

"Billy, we can't sell out. Let me talk to Stephan, my fiancé," I pleaded. "He's rich. I'm sure he can help us."

"No, Cat, no," Billy argued. "It's not fair to you. This is business, not personal. And what if he thinks you're a gold digger?"

"Billy's right. You don't want to jeopardize your relationship," India agreed. "You don't know how Stephan will react. And you finally got what you wanted, Cat. I wouldn't want you to lose it.

"Don't be so glum, Billy, we can always go back to what we did before," she added.

"What was that?" I asked, intrigued.

"Run an escort agency from his apartment."

"Oh!" I said, remembering my first visit.

Billy didn't laugh. If this mysterious investor bought out *Arbiteur*, it was certain he would insist we move our offices—and that was a situation he faced with horror. After all, it would mean he would have to leave his apartment.

When I arrived home, I decided to tell Stephan about *Arbiteur* right away. Even if India and Billy had entreated me not to sour my chances of being the future Princess of Westonia, I knew that Stephan would do anything to help. As for the preposterous accusation Brick Winthrop had leveled—what rubbish. He was probably just jealous Stephan had a title and he didn't.

"Stephan darling," I said, when I entered the loft, "I need to—"

"There's someone here," Stephan said.

"Oh. But, I wanted to ask—"

"I think you need to speak to him right now," Stephan said ominously.

"All right, but . . ."

I walked into the room to find a dark-suited man with mirrored sunglasses inspecting the exposed beams on the ceiling and the wires hanging down to the floor. He looked vaguely familiar—then it hit me. My stalker! Of course. But why was he inside the apartment? Why had Stephan let him in?

"Hello?"

"Miss McAllister?"

"Yes."

"Is a Bannerjee Bunsdaraat at this address?"

"Yes. But what does that have to do with anything? Didn't Heidi send you?"

"Heidi who?"

"My publicist and image consultant. You're a stalker, aren't you?"

"No. I work for the INS."

"The INS?"

"Yes. We've been scouting the location and keeping close tabs on Miss Bunsdaraat."

"You were stalking *Bannerjee?*" I asked, disappointed. So I didn't even have my own stalker—my au pair did. Very off-putting indeed.

"In a manner of speaking, yes. Actually we were just making sure she didn't go anywhere until we got the proper documentation for her arrest."

"Banny's a criminal?" I asked excitedly. I didn't know she had it in her!

"Not exactly, but she will have to come with us."

"Why?"

"Miss Bunsdaraat is an illegal alien. She used a fake visa to return to the United States."

"A fake visa! I paid good money for that visa on Fulton Street!" I argued.

"Miss McAllister, nobody has a right to *sell* or *buy* a visa. You can only apply for one at the U.S. embassy."

"That's what I told India—but she said it would take too long! That's why I went to Fulton Street!"

"It doesn't make a difference now. Miss Bunsdaraat should

never have been allowed to return to the United States and must be deported back to Sri Lanka immediately."

"What?"

"We're going to have to do a search of the area," he said, showing me a warrant for Bannerjee's deportation. "Let's go, boys." He stood aside as a veritable SWAT team in full riot gear entered our apartment.

"Banny!" I called. Perhaps I could warn her before they closed in on her location. *Run, Banny, run!*

"What's going on?" Stephan asked.

"They've come to take Bannerjee away!" I said, trembling with agitation.

The SWAT team searched every bit of the loft—even the fake ceilings, the numerous trapdoors, and the portable coolers. Since it was such a wide-open space, there was little room for a one hundred-pound, five-foot Sri Lankan au pair to hide. Except . . .

"She's obviously not here," I said triumphantly, standing in front of the temperature-controlled closet and discreetly manipulating the lock's retina controls. There was no way they would be able to get in there now!

"What's this?" A SWAT team member in a bulletproof helmet, his finger cocked on the trigger of his AK-47, asked.

"Nothing. It's just a—"

"Stand back, ma'am."

"Noooooooooo!" I screamed, horrified beyond belief. My mother's living legacy! My racks and racks of unworn designer clothes! It had survived Brother Parish, it would certainly survive a SWAT team! Plus, Bannerjee was most likely hiding inside in a Louis Vuitton trunk! "Stephan! Stephan! Darling, help me!" I called as I attempted to handcuff myself to the closet door. With Stephan's assistance I was able to chain myself to the handle with a chain-link Chanel logo belt. Unfortunately, the INS officer was able to pulverize the knot with a precise beam of his laser-controlled AK-47. I fell to the ground, my wrist smoking.

The INS officer blasted the lock on the door and began a thorough search inside. I cursed them all. "Bastards! This is the U.S.A.! You can't do this! You can't!" Stephan attempted to tackle the officer to the ground, but was quickly dispatched with a drop-kick karate chop.

Cries of pain and agony could be heard as the SWAT team invaded my closet—but it was only because all the racks of shoe boxes and fur storage bins had crashed down upon their heads.

"Sir! We've got something!" a hairy combatant finally yelled. He had found Banny cowering behind my collection of Liberace Russian czar costumes.

"Aieeeeeeee!" Bannerjee screamed as the INS agents led her out in handcuffs.

"Banny!" I cried in despair. Where would I ever find an au pair like Bannerjee? Who would meticulously catalog my wardrobe according to designer or dead celebrity now? Who would know the difference between Voyage and Valentino? Fake London and Custo Barcelona? Branquinho and Balenciaga? Victor & Rolf and Dolce & Gabbna? Ossie Clark and Oscar de la Renta? Pucci and Gucci?

"Miss Cat! Help me!" she called. I ran down to watch as they stuffed poor Bannerjee in the backseat of a shuttle van and drove her away.

"What the hell was that all about?" Stephan asked, scratching his head.

"They've taken Bannerjee! She's an illegal alien!" I cried in despair.

◊

Tracking down a detained illegal alien was harder than I thought. Several phone calls to the INS resulted in my being transferred to several detention centers. I was bounced from Cuban to Haitian to Cambodian fugitives before I finally found out that Bannerjee was being held in a small room near Kennedy Airport. "Bannerjee Bunsdaraat," the official said. "Yes. Her deportation trial is in a few hours."

"Is there any way I can see her?"

"Yes, she is allowed one visitor."

I arrived to find the INS offices a despicable affair. First of all, I had to wait in a maze of lines that stretched down the block. Once inside the building, another long line of plastic seats awaited us. A clerk in the front handed you a number, which was flashed on several screens around the dingy office. It was just like the DMV—not that I know how to drive. If you missed your number, you had to go to the back of the line. I watched the screen with rapt attention, dutifully shuffling from one seat to another, until I finally reached the front, only to be told I had been waiting in the wrong line all along.

"You're here for a green card application?" the INS officer asked me.

"No, I'm here to see an illegal alien," I explained.

"Oh. You don't have to wait in line for that," she sniffed, and pointed me toward the detention center on the other side of the room.

Bannerjee was waiting for me in a lockdown. Her hair was matted and frizzy, and instead of her typical Marc Jacobs apron dress that served as her uniform, they had put her in a gray jumpsuit.

"Miss Cat! Miss Cat!" she cried. "I so sorry!"

"It's not your fault, Banny," I said. "Don't worry, we'll get you out of here! It's all my fault—I shouldn't have sent you to China! I feel terrible. There must be some way to keep you in the country."

"There is. My caseworker said you testify at trial and say I an immigrant with special skills."

"Is that all! Of course I will!" I said benevolently.

"Thank you, Miss Cat."

I returned in an hour, all set to *testilie* in dear Banny's deportation trial. I had taken a muscle-relaxing drug procured from Dr. Feel-nothing to beat the lie detector test, and was shocked to realize there was no such machine in the courtroom. Apparently just swearing on a Bible that I was telling the truth, the whole truth, and nothing but was enough. No electroshock necessary. Well! In that case, the prosecution would be better off having me swear on a stack of Italian *Vogue* magazines.

I raised my right hand in preparation and looked around at the small room, which held four people: the immigration judge, the prosecuting attorney, the public defender, and Bannerjee.

"Miss Bunsdaraat was in your employ for how long?"

"Six months," I answered truthfully.

"And in those six months, did she display any special skills?" the prosecutor asked leadingly.

"Oh, yes," I replied eagerly. "I even sent Banny away to the Ivor Spencer International School for Butler Administrators and Personal Assistants."

"What is that?"

"It's the leading domestic-help agency in London, which has a training course for personal assistants."

"And what did she learn there?"

"Rudimentary tasks demanded in the high-stress position of personal assistant to a high-profile, ahem, celebrity. Helicopter lessons, organizational management of social calendars, advanced RSVP."

"I see. And did Miss Bunsdaraat use what she had learned in this course?"

"Of course!"

"Tell me, Miss McAllister. During the time Miss Bunsdaraat was in your employ, was the laundry ever done?"

"Well . . ."

"Answer the question."

I was flustered. "Well, most of my clothes don't really need to be laundered," I hedged, thinking of the piles of dry cleaning.

The prosecutor grunted. "As for your affairs, would you say she kept them in order?"

"Oh, indisputably," I said. In my mind, Bannerjee was right up there with Michael Jackson's llama keeper and Courtney Cox's dentist. It wouldn't be long before *Entertainment Weekly* listed Bannerjee in its "Top 100 Service Providers." I was sure Bannerjee would receive even more fan mail than Richard Dreyfuss's house-keeper, who eloquently said to her employer, "You don't enjoy your life as much as I do."

"But during your twenty-fifth birthday party—"

"Yes?"

"Isn't it true that Miss Bunsdaraat was not available to help you find something to wear?"

"Well, it was a last-minute thing, really. I did have something to wear, I just wanted to change," I explained.

"And because you were not able to change into something else, isn't it true, Miss McAllister, that you were almost not allowed into your own birthday party?"

"It's true. But it was my fault!" I argued.

"And as for advanced RSVP, isn't it true that you usually find yourself at parties or fashion shows to which Miss Bunsdaraat has ostensibly RSVP'd, only to find when you arrive at the event that your name was not on the list?"

"But that doesn't prove anything—"

"And isn't it true, Miss McAllister, that Miss Bunsdaraat does not have any idea how to take care of a baby? And is not in the least bit qualified to take care of children?" he thundered.

"No, no, of course not. Boing loves Banny!"

"Exhibit A, Your Honor," the prosecutor said, passing along a faded yellow Post-it note. "May I show it to the witness?"

The judge grunted his assent.

I took the note from the prosecutor.

"Tell me, Miss McAllister, is this in your handwriting?"

I scanned it, my heart sinking. "Yes."

"If it please the court, will you read what is written on the note?"

"Do I have to?" I pleaded.

"Miss McAllister, please read the note," the judge ordered.

I sighed, reading from the Post-it. " 'Banny darling, if it's not too much to ask, could we please feed Boing today?' "

"Silence! Silence!" the judge barked, although the only noise was my and Bannerjee's whimpers.

"I rest my case, Your Honor. Bannerjee Bunsdaraat is an illegal alien with no special skills, domestic or otherwise, to contribute to American society."

"She can catalog an entire fashion wardrobe," I interrupted defensively. "She knows how to take care of Martin Margiela sweaters with unfinished hems! She can spot a fake Rolex from a mile away! She's extremely talented!"

The judge decided. "That doesn't count."

"No?"

"No. Miss Bunsdaraat has been proven as a leech on society with no special skills as a domestic helper, a personal assistant, or as a nanny."

I gave Banny an imploring look, and she slumped in her chair.

"Deportation date is set for tomorrow," the judge ordered.

Bannerjee was escorted out in handcuffs. When I got home, I sent Mummy another cablegram, hoping this one would reach her in Timbuktu. After all, it had been Mummy's idea that I hire Bannerjee—Mummy would be worried about her welfare. Plus, if I didn't stop Banny from being deported, who would look after my clothes? Or Boing? Or me?

23. *the princess bride*

When I returned, I was determined to have that conversation with Stephan. If he loved me, he wouldn't think I was a gold digger, would he? Nevertheless, I simply had no choice. There was a company to save, a boss to keep out of jail, and an au pair to rescue from deportation. His bazillions would come in handy, oh, just about now. I found him in the middle of the room, singing softly to the baby.

"Darling?" I said. "Can we have a moment?"

"Oh, of course," he said. "Should I put Boing back in her coat?"

"Yes, that would be good."

He picked up the baby and put her back gently in the duvet. "Well?"

"I was thinking . . . you know your bazillions?"

"My what?"

"Well—your money. I need it," I blurted.

"Oh." His eyes widened.

"I need to pay a lawyer to stop Bannerjee from being deported, and to defend *Arbiteur* from a crippling lawsuit," I explained. "Otherwise Billy's going to jail, or we're selling off *Arbiteur* and India can't be a part of it, and I can't allow that to happen because India's friendship means the world to me, and . . . and . . ."

"But why do you need *my* money?" he asked.

"Because . . . well, I don't have any."

"You don't?" He gagged.

"No."

"What do you mean you don't? I thought—"

"What?"

"That you were famous. You knew Cece and Teeny. They're the two richest women in Manhattan."

"Yeesss . . . I do. I went to grammar school with them. That was a long time ago."

"But the penthouse?"

"I leased it at my accountant's behest. I couldn't afford to live there anymore."

"What about all the photographers during Fashion Week? Front row at all the fashion shows?"

"I upgraded my seat."

"You . . . what did you say?"

"Upgraded my seat," I repeated.

"Why?"

"Because I only got standing room, that's why," I said crossly.

"But you said you didn't have to work."

"I lied."

"You lied?"

"I don't. Have. Money. I'm bankrupt. I was working for *Arbiteur* and we were all set to have an IPO and make gazillions but then Catwalk.com threatened to sue us for stealing their streaming video coverage and our bankers dropped our IPO and now I'm broke. But now someone wants to buy the website—but only for a million dollars, which is insane, especially since we're in debt for much more than that—but even if we sell it to them, they don't want India to be part of it, which of course we can't let happen because she's my very best friend in the whole world."

"Oh." He looked perplexed. "But I thought—"

"Darling," I said, a thought forming in my head. "Where is Westonia?"

"It's . . . umm . . . in the Baltic," he hedged.

"I thought it was in the Balkans?"

"It isn't. At least, I don't think it is."

"Are you sure?"

"Am I sure of what?"

Trembling, I reached for his eye patch.

"What—what are you doing?" he asked fearfully.

I took his eye patch . . . and I moved it to the other eye. Then I remembered—whenever I saw him at Barneys, his eye patch was on the left eye. Whenever I saw him out at social events, it was on the right. It had been a clever disguise, because even if anyone he met on the social circuit bumped into him at Barneys, he or she would never have recognized him—most of the crowd were too narcissistic to notice.

"I can explain," he said in a completely unambiguous Continental accent—except it came from this continent. The northern one.

"Explain what?"

"I'm not the Prince of Westonia."

"Of course you're not," I said dully.

"I'm a tailor at Barneys."

"I know."

"You do?"

"Brick finally remembered how he knew you."

"Ah. I wondered when he would. He was a good customer."

"But you were at that twenty-thousand-dollars-a-plate benefit . . ."

"Cece paid for my ticket. I told her my accounts hadn't been set up yet."

"And all those parties . . ."

"You should know as well as I do that it's very easy to score party invitations. After all, I worked at Barneys and I had—"

"The Fashion Calendar?"

He nodded.

"And the fashion shows?"

"I told you, a friend invited me. And I was in Paris to pick up some new fabric for our custom-made suits."

"But Sun Valley, the moguls . . ."

"That was a little harder. One of my clients had left his invitation in a coat pocket I was altering, so I pinched it."

"Brick!" I said, remembering how sore Brick had been about not being invited to Sun Valley this year.

"Yes. It was his ticket. I knew you were going to be at that retreat, and I wanted to see you."

"But how did you—"

"Infiltrate? Dupe the crème de la crème of New York society?" He laughed. "I'm a paparazzo. I worked in Europe for years taking photographs of the jet set. I know all their tricks. I decided, why should they have all the fun?"

"Why, indeed."

"I found this site on the Internet, E-Royalty-to-Go.com," he explained. "For a hundred ninety-nine dollars you can buy yourself a title. Any title. European. Middle Eastern. Whatever. It's like those sites where you can buy university degrees even though you've never attended one of those schools."

"Yes, I know of them."

"Well, that's what I got. And since I recognized everyone from society, I just ingratiated myself to one of the more gullible socialites."

"Cece Phipps-Langley."

"Yes. I didn't even have to tell her anything—I just said I was an exiled prince and she just assumed—"

"Homes in Baden-Baden? Beverly Hills? Bedford?"

"Yes."

"But when I saw you, you said you lived on Fifth Avenue."

"I did. On Fifth Avenue and East One Hundred and Tenth Street."

"East One Hundred and Tenth! Isn't that—"

"The camera obscura apartment," he said wistfully.

"I thought it was your studio!"

"Yes, in a sense it was, but I got evicted last week," he explained sheepishly.

"So what *do* you have?"

"Well, when my parents died, I inherited their farmhouse in Michigan."

"A landowner," I sniped.

"Cat—please, don't be upset."

"Upset? Why would I be upset? The only job I've ever had is gone, and the only man I've ever loved turns out to be from *Michigan.*" Flyoverland. The horror, the horror!

"Is that so bad?"

"Please leave."

"But where will I go?"

"I don't care," I said, all steely-like. "Just get out of my sight. I can't stand . . . I can't . . . oh God . . ." I crumpled, thinking of the humiliation in store for me.

Stephan left.

It began as soon as I opened my eyes. For a while there, I thought it was all just a bad, bad dream. But then I had to answer the phone. It was India.

"Cat! Have you seen the papers?" she asked breathlessly.

"Is it a story about Stephan and my engagement?" I groaned.

"Well, yes."

"And?"

"Cat, he's an impostor! He's not a prince at all!" India cried.

"I know. He told me last night," I said. "How bad is it?"

"Well, let's just put it this way—*no one's ever going to forget you now.*"

I padded out to my doorway to collect the heap of newspapers and tabloids.

"Prince of Lies!" the *Post* trumpeted. "The Con Artist Formerly Known as the Prince"—that from the *Daily News*. The *Times* had run a small mention in "Public Lives," in its usual restrained fashion. *New York* magazine had the full story, which included nasty asides from several well-heeled anonymous socialites who had welcomed "the Prince of Westonia" into their homes and were now counting the silver and making sure nothing had been stolen. Teeny Wong Finklestein Van der Hominie was quoted as saying she had known all along that he was a fake, as he didn't play polo nor did he know how to sail. The paper also mentioned that Teeny was planning a million-dollar wedding in Malibu to billionaire polo-playing venture capitalist Brockton Moorehouse Winthrop the Third. Apparently she had been successful in that venture as well.

I rang Heidi to see if there was any way to combat this egregious affair. I'd call a press conference! I'd give teary interviews! I'd play the woman wronged! I'd . . . I'd . . . Heidi wasn't picking up the phone and when she did, she did not sound pleased to hear from me.

"Vooo eezz dees?" she asked suspiciously.

"Heidi, it's me, Cat."

"Vooo?"

"Cat."

"I zon't know a Caf," she said darkly.

"Heidi, please, you've got to help me."

Reluctantly, Heidi told me it was the worst press she had seen in years. "And, yes, there ees soch a theeng as bad press, Caf."

All the magazines, television shows, and newspapers were now begging to talk to me, of course—not because I was engaged to a prince, but because I was the fiancée of a fool. Instead of puffy profiles dedicated to my wedding trousseau and whirlwind romance, I would now be described as the hopeless debutante dupe who had fallen for a hustler. It was terrible. Already I had been bumped off the committees to fight colitis and aggravated bowel movements. Even the Dumpster Disaster in the Philippines committee didn't want me. I was worse than trash.

Photographers were stalking my loft. Boing and I were besieged at every turn, and I hid out in *Arbiteur* HQ, the only safe place from the prying eyes of the media monster. Billy was sympathetic when I told him the news.

"Well, it's not like it's a crime," Billy argued. He was very touchy about what was and wasn't illegal these days.

"Impersonating a prince? I suppose not," I agreed, cheering up.

"Well, the investors have sent over the papers," Billy said glumly.

"So that's it? We're just giving up?" I asked.

"I mean, India can't stay mad forever, can she?" Billy asked. "What else can we do?"

"Nothing—absolutely nothing," I lamented.

When I arrived home, I found Stephan in the apartment. I had forgotten we had agreed for him to collect his things that afternoon.

"Well, it was fun while it lasted," he said. "I guess I'll be going back to my acre in Michigan now. Or I could go back to shooting for the *Globe*. I'm sure Princess Caroline misses me."

"Right."

He looked so forlorn, standing against the wall. He wasn't even wearing the eye patch anymore—what was the point? He was no longer a dashing exiled Westonian prince but just another unmasked social upstart. At least Andrew Cunanan went out in a blaze of attention-grabbing glory. We would have to live through ours.

"OK."

"OK."

He headed over to the door.

"Wait."

He turned back and looked at me expectantly.

"Nothing." I shrugged. "I thought you had maybe forgotten something."

"Oh." He sighed.

Suddenly I realized the pain I was feeling was not from every hurtful headline or gleefully wicked investigative piece or even the newest revelation from the Smoking Gun website that Stephan had attended agriculture school. He turned away and I noticed, not for the first time, how broad his shoulders were and how nice his profile was. I remembered how kind he had been the first time we had met, and how he was staunchly on the side of beleaguered party crashers everywhere—a perverse kindness to be sure, but still a generosity of spirit that was rare in me-first Manhattan. He was the only man who saw the crazy world I lived in for what it was— upside down and backward. Besides, he even had the good humor to put up with a woman who named her adopted child Boing and lived in a converted campground. I didn't just love Stephan. I liked him. And he liked me, which was even more important, really.

"Wait," I said again. "Don't go."

"Gee, Cat, I didn't know you really cared," he said, smiling shyly.

Neither did I. But, hell, who really wanted to be rich and famous anyway? Look what happened when Diana married a real prince. There was more to life than being a princess. Did I really want to end up throwing myself at international playboys for the rest of my life?

"So what are we going to do now?" I asked Stephan, snuggling into his arms.

"I don't know . . . move to Michigan?" he joked.

"Well, it's not a bad idea," I said, contemplating the thought. "We could justify it by saying we've given up on the rat race and have decided to live life on a simpler, more monastic level. You know, like all those lawyers who become chefs, or investment bankers who leave Wall Street to surf in Maui. Everyone is moving to Nebraska or Wisconsin or Montana, anyhow," I mused. "Like Demi Moore—she's in Idaho. Or Ted Turner; he's in Montana. And Todd Oldham is in Pennsylvania. All those models are living in the Catskills. Even Donovan Leitch lives in the countryside." Slowly, I was warming to the idea. I could subscribe to all those new magazines that advocated the simple life—like *Simplycity* and *Real Simple*. Of course! New York was *so* over. How had I not noticed this before?

"It's always got to be a trend for you, doesn't it?" Stephan teased.

"Of course, darling! Otherwise, why even live?" I asked, perking up at the thought of being at the forefront of stylish country living.

We celebrated by going back to Barneys, Boing in tow. It was rather romantic, when you thought about it. Stephan's old colleagues in the made-to-measure department all came out to shake his hand and take souvenir photographs. I'd never been to the fifth floor of Barneys, and it was quite an eye-opener. It was a completely sober suit shop, and looked more like Brooks Brothers than Barneys. There were no purple sweaters. No poofy coats. No vinyl jeans. And that was the men's department I was thinking of. The old-school tailors with their silver hair and perpetually bent backs who worked there were probably the only straight men working in the entire store.

"Never knew we had a prince in here," one of them said jovially.

"Stephan, he is a nice boy," another told me.

"And not a bad tailor."

When they were finished saying good-bye to Stephan, I spent the last of my money on a Comme des Garçons apron dress. Provincial chic!

24. deus ex mummy-na

The streets of Tribeca were desolate and quiet when we returned from our uptown shopping exodus. I began to feel a little pang at the thought of abandoning the city. Stephan and Boing were silent as well, as if they also felt it—a darkened feeling of failure. Whenever people left the city, it was never for something better, and it was always with a sense of defeat. Whether to Hollywood or Des Moines, it was all the same—leaving New York meant that you couldn't cut it, you hadn't made it, you were getting out before it was too late, and that although you were living in a city where anything could happen, somehow, nothing had ever happened to you.

For once there were no stray photographers milling about our doorstep, as our prominence as the most scandal-plagued couple of the week took a backseat to the *earth-shattering* news that model agency executives were sleeping with their underage clients. We took the freight elevator up to the top floor and nodded to neighbors we passed on our way. Stephan pulled the elevator door open and I fumbled with the keys, only to discover the door was already unlocked. The sound of cheerful voices and tinkling glass floated from the middle of the room, and I was shocked to find I was treading on a nice Aubusson rug, and hearing the sound of Billie Holiday crooning on the sound system. What was this? Stephan and I exchanged puzzled looks, and drew nearer with a mixture of apprehension and excitement.

In the middle of the room, a close approximation of a sitting room had been assembled. A deep, berry-rich rug covered the grim wooden planks. The Martin Margiela duvet had been folded into a dry-cleaning bag, replaced by a delightful English pram; the electrical cords hanging from the ceiling were obscured with sparkling Christmas lights; and the overwhelming sense of *nouveau* disrepair had given way to a cozy atmosphere of properly faded gentility. Two overstuffed Queen Anne armchairs crowded around a mahogany coffee table, where two women were in the process of mixing cocktails.

"India!" I cried, recognizing one of the uninvited guests. "What's going on?"

India looked up with a mischievous gleam in her eye, and nudged her companion, who turned to face us.

"DARLING!" cried a small woman, wearing a gigantic turban and a salwar kameez, her spread arms jangling dozens of familiar ruby-encrusted bracelets; in one hand was an ivory cigarette holder, in the other, a martini glass.

"Oh my God. MUMMY!" I cried, running toward her.

We kissed and hugged each other effusively, as if we hadn't seen each other in years . . . which we hadn't. Stephan grinned from the sidelines, holding Boing, who was cooing appreciatively at the multicolored expanse of Mummy's outfit.

"What's going on? How did you get here? Why didn't you tell me?" I asked.

"Sweetheart, what have you done to your hair this time?" she asked, tut-tutting at my new coif, then said, "I was trying to reach you, sweetie." She smoothed my sweater and patted my hair. "I kept receiving all these distressing cablegrams from you, following me across the globe. But every time I called the penthouse, some strange woman would hang up the phone," she explained. "You never told me you'd moved!"

"But how did you find out?" I asked.

"India," Mummy said simply.

India looked up modestly. "Martini?" she asked Stephan, who nodded. She passed me a glass as well. "I had overheard Teeny saying something about a crazy woman prank-calling her apartment. She seemed very annoyed about it, and was complaining to this telecommunications billionaire to see if there was anything she could do to block the calls. Apparently her Caller ID always identified a different international number. Anyway, she finally had the calls traced and they weren't from a telephone at all, but a very sophisticated international Palm Pilot e-mail/phone."

"But how did you know the calls were for me?" I asked, mystified.

"The caller was always asking for someone named "Norma-Jean," India replied.

I blushed pink. Norma-Jean was my real name, but only my mother called me that. My agent had dubbed me Cat. Mummy never approved of the change, as she thought stage names were hopelessly tacky.

"I was terrifically worried, Norma-Jean," Mummy said. "You shouldn't worry Mummy like that!"

"But how did you track her down, India?" I asked, turning to my friend, who was looking very pleased with herself.

"Remember that CEO who was very partial to my charms?" she asked.

"The one who twirled you around so you looked like a Mexican piñata?"

"The one and only." India nodded. "Well, I asked him about these newfangled international-dialing Palm Pilots and he told me it was very easy to find out who had one, as they were not on the market yet, and had been given to a very elite group. I asked him if he could get me the list, and he said why not. At that point, he was very drunk. He called the office and found out there were only three people on the list: himself, Bill Gates, and—"

"Me," Mummy said, blushing pink. "Because I travel so much."

"Oh, Mummy, you're actually here!" I enthused.

"Yes. I've missed New York." Mummy nodded. "It's good to be home. But what's this I hear? You're bankrupt? Again?"

I nodded. I told Mummy everything—how my trust fund had run out, but how I had found fulfilling employment at *Arbiteur*, the promise of stock options, the threat of a lawsuit from Catwalk.com, the mysterious investor who had offered to buy *Arbiteur* for a paltry million-dollar settlement, and how I was now moving to Michigan.

"Michigan?" Mummy gasped. "Why on earth?"

"Oh, I'm sorry—Mummy, this is Stephan. He used to be the Prince of Westonia, but he isn't anymore."

Mummy offered Stephan her hand, which he kissed gallantly. "Pleased to make your acquaintance, Mrs. McAllister."

She gave Stephan a dismissive wave. "Please, call me Mummy. Everyone does."

"OK, Mummy."

"And why on earth is Catwalk.com suing *Arbiteur*?"

"For stealing their streaming video," I explained, abashed. "I had forgotten to bring our digital video camera to Fashion Week."

"Dear, dear." Mummy sighed. "You always were a forgetful child." She gave me a perturbed look and crossed her arms. "Now, who is this investor who's offering to buy your company for a million dollars?"

"We don't really know. Some sort of apparel company. They promised they'd be able to handle the Catwalk.com lawsuit. I don't know why they're so set on buying us out. It's not like we have anything to offer aside from our press credentials at Fashion Week."

"Press credentials? Why would an apparel company need press credentials?" Stephan asked.

"I don't know." I shrugged.

"Wait—did you say they were interested in our press credentials?" India asked, intrigued.

"Yes, they kept asking Billy if it was true that we got invitations to all the fashion shows," I said.

"And they're an apparel company?" India repeated.

"You don't think . . ." I said, finally catching on.

"Of course I do!"

"Tart Tarteen! Teeny's behind it all!" I concluded. "Of course! She's been banned from all the fashion shows for stealing their designs!"

"Come to think of it, that's why she kept inviting me to all those fashion shows," Stephan said.

"She was the 'friend'?"

"Yes," he said angrily. "She wanted me there and asked me to take notes. She said she was too busy to go, and I did it as a favor."

"She was also at MogulFest," I added. "She must have heard me talking to people about *Arbiteur* there."

"It all makes sense," India said. "Especially since they were demanding editorial control."

"They wanted to convince our audience of fashion fanatics to give up the real thing for her despicably shameless riffs on true artistic fashion inspiration! Polyester for silk! Pleather pants! Acrylic sweaters! Oh, how awful!"

"Tsk, tsk." Mummy shook her head. "Despicable, indeed."

"But even if we don't sell out to Teeny, there's still the Catwalk.com lawsuit," I said.

Just then, Mummy's spanking-new international Palm Pilot began to beep. Mummy flipped it open and put it to her ear. "Hello? Hello?" she asked. "I can't hear you." She shook the device crossly. "You know, this has never worked quite the same ever since that horrid Hong Kong flu. I lost all my datafiles, all my phone numbers, all my—"

Stephan pounced. "The Hong Kong flu! I lost all the information on my computer as well!"

"So did all of *Arbiteur*'s computers!" I said, remembering.

"It wiped databases clean on all nine continents!" India extolled.

"Which means—"

"Catwalk.com doesn't have a shred of evidence!" I cheered.

"Not one pixel!" India whooped.

Mummy looked up from her apparatus; she was attempting to punch Star 69 with her stylus, trying to find out whose call she had missed. "Hhmmmm? What is it, dears?"

"Mummy—you've saved us!" I cried, dancing around her, linking hands with India and Stephan, while Boing clucked happily.

"I have?" Mummy asked.

"Yes!"

"That's why we were approached by that mysterious investor right when we got back from Sun Valley!" India surmised. "They knew Catwalk.com didn't have a case, and they knew they could buy *Arbiteur* on the cheap!"

"Which means—" I said.

"We're back!" India crowed.

"I have my job back!" I screamed. "*Arbiteur* isn't going down the tubes!"

"We've got to call Billy to tell him that he doesn't have to sell the company or go to jail! *Arbiteur* is saved!" I cheered. India immediately called Billy to tell him the good news.

"But what about Bannerjee?" I suddenly remembered. "They're about to deport her!"

"Bannerjee? That sweet girl I sent to look after you?" Mummy asked. "Why are they deporting her?"

"Because she's an illegal alien, Mum," I explained. "She shouldn't have been working in this country."

"What should she have been doing?"

"I don't know, being a tourist, I suppose. Going to the Empire State Building. Riding around in one of those double-decker buses."

"Oh."

*   *   *

I ushered everyone into the town car—a squeeze given the number of us; for once I wished I had a stretch limousine on hand—and we journeyed to the deportation center.

"Wait, wait!" I said, when I saw they were leading Bannerjee out of the cell into a waiting INS car to take her to the airport and send her to her fishing village in Sri Lanka. I had no idea how we were going to save Bannerjee, but India came through again.

"I have the written testimony from a very good character witness who can attest to Bannerjee's special skills," India declared.

"You do?" I gaped. Would wonders never cease?

She nodded. "While you were busy mooning over Stephan here, I was researching our defense." India pulled out an official-looking letter on heavy parchment that bore a wax seal and handed it to the INS official.

"To whom it may concern," he read. "This is to testify that Miss Bannerjee Bunsdaraat is of sound mind and body and is judged to have great character and very, very, special skills." He gasped. "It's signed—"

"Prince William!" India proclaimed. "Isn't he such a nice boy?"

The INS official, like most of the American public, was enraptured by the idea of the British royal family, and ordered an immediate reassessment of Bannerjee's case. He was so impressed by our royal connections he released her right away.

We returned to the refurbished loft, happy and exhausted. Mummy settled back into her armchair and looked around. "I still haven't been formally introduced to my grandchild," she said, holding her arms out for Boing.

"Mummy, this is Boing," I said. "Boing, meet Grandmummy."

"Boing?" Mummy asked. "What a strange name for such an adorable baby." She held Boing protectively in her lap.

"Miss Cat—what did you say? Her name is not Boing." Bannerjee interjected.

"What do you mean?" I asked, slightly offended. "That's what you told me in the airport—that her name was Boing. I assumed it was a sacred Chinese name."

Bannerjee laughed. "No, no, no, her name is not Boing," she explained. "Her birth parents wanted to name her after great American city."

"And?"

"Her name is Boyne. B-O-Y-N-E," Banny said.

"Boyne?"

"That's right. *Boyne*. Like *coin*."

"What great American city is Boyne?" I asked. "I've never heard of it."

"Ahem." Stephan coughed.

We all looked up at him expectantly.

"I know where Boyne is. It's in Michigan," he explained. "Where *I'm* from."

the after-party

25. the return of the park avenue princess

Mummy didn't dash off this time, and we spent several glorious days shopping, lunching, and generally having the time of our lives. She was always so much fun wherever we went—although she was so loud we always got kicked out of the more reputable establishments we patronized.

Once the lawsuit against *Arbiteur* was properly dismissed, and Billy assured us that any threat of prosecution was highly unlikely, I was back at my usual work space—the leather couch across from Billy's desk. India was perched in her usual position as well, on the armrest of the couch.

"I'm so glad!" Billy said. "This couldn't have come at a better time!"

I gave Billy a triumphant smile; India grinned happily.

"Now that we're not going out of business after all and our credit line has been reinstated," Billy said, "I thought it was high time I gave you girls a raise." India and I began hooting, but Billy wasn't finished. "And I thought, why not move our offices somewhere more spacious?"

"Billy—no—you're actually going to—"

"Leave your apartment?" I asked, thinking I had just the right replacement.

"Why, yes," he said. I suddenly noticed Billy wasn't wearing his usual tank top and pajama bottoms. Also, he was clean-shaven. He wore a sharp black Gucci suit and polished wing tips. "I thought it was time for a change."

Billy moved *Arbiteur*'s offices to my newly vacated Tribeca loft. With the raise he had given me, I was able to kick Teeny out of my Park Avenue penthouse and move back to the family homestead pronto.

There were two new additions to the *Arbiteur* staff: Bannerjee, for one. *Arbiteur* was now sponsoring her work visa, and she was the official videographer for the site. Since she was on the masthead, she even started to receive party invitations herself.

As for Boing, she finally said her first word.

"GUCCI!" the baby chortled when she would see me. "GUCCI GUCCI GUCCI!"

I was so proud.

Mummy left for the Balkans—or the Baltic, I can never remember—but promised to come back to visit this summer, when Stephan and I will repair to our country home in Boyne, Michigan. Since Stephan wasn't a Westonian prince, he wasn't at all related to Catherine Oxenberg, although strangely enough, we did a little research on his family tree and found out he was third cousins twice removed from her husband—Casper *Van* Diem.

Stephan and I have yet to become one of Manhattan's golden couples—the ones who suck up all the energy in certain rooms, causing heads to swivel and photographers to angle for the best shot. But what we have been able to do is turn a room in the penthouse into another camera obscura, so that every time New York gets to be too much, we can remember that life here is best viewed upside down and backward. A gallery has even expressed interest in showing Stephan's work. Apparently we're not the only ones who like to look at the city from a different angle.

Heidi took me back as a client and informed me that I might have a new career opportunity as well. Apparently Barneys had finally noticed that I was one of their biggest customers; awed by my impressive shopping skills, they wanted to sign me up to appear in their next advertising campaign: "Spend Your Heart Out—with Cat McAllister."

And it was the time of year again to plan my birthday party. I called Heidi, India, and Bannerjee in for a meeting.

"This year," I said, "I'm thinking I'm not going to celebrate my twenty-fifth birthday for the fifth time," I announced.

"Vous not?" Heidi gasped, her fountain pen slipping through her fingers.

"No, I think I'm too old for that." I chuckled.

"Wow, does that mean you're actually going to celebrate your thir—" India asked.

"My twenty-*sixth* birthday, for the *first* time," I said, cutting her off quickly. "Now, I was thinking, where should we have it? That deserted airline hangar? Or perhaps that deconsecrated synagogue on the Lower East Side? Do you think Chloe Sevigny will make it?"

about the author

MELISSA DE LA CRUZ is a senior fashion editor at *hintmag.com*, and has contributed to print and online publications, including *Allure*, *The New York Times*, *New York Press*, *Feed*, and *Nerve*. She grew up in Manila and San Francisco, and graduated from Columbia University. She lives in New York City.

KIM DEMARCO is an illustrator whose work appears in *The New Yorker* and *The New York Times*. Her clients have included Barneys New York, Visionaire, and the New York Public Library. Kim lives in New York City, where she is on the faculty of the Parsons School of Design.